For all who've had a vampire phase and those who've never outgrown it.

Prologue

It Simply Started

It's been two years since the vampires emerged and seized control. All that remained remembered the chaos and bloodshed like it was yesterday when the first pale creatures with glistening fangs appeared seemingly overnight. Panic swept across the globe as they slaughtered without mercy or restraint.

In mere months, humanity was crushed under the heel of its new immortal overlords. Old governments and ways of life were demolished. The vampires swiftly built new settlements mimicking human towns, but it was only a facade of civility masking the barbarity lurking beneath.

Now people live in constant fear, nervous when pale figures with burning red eyes will emerge from the shadows to feed. Most cower and obey, but there are whispered tales of a fledgling resistance plotting to somehow overthrow the bloodthirsty tyrants.

But the greatest tragedy is what happened to the women - the darkest stain on the vampires' savage reign. Many young girls were ripped from their families and forced into gilded cages called Nests. There they are trained and collared to being Blood Brides betrothed to the monsters themselves.

At night, they are fed on until passing out from blood loss, only to be healed by a few drops of their masters' blood come morning. It is a never-ending cycle of horror that withers the soul. The only comfort is the sisterhood forged between Brides as they cling to their humanity.

They are the Blood Brides - both prisoners and warriors in spirit. We tell their hidden stories so that those who come after understand what they sacrificed for hope.

Chapter One

Learning How to Live

The light bled through, and Helena Swanson knew it was time to die.

Her eyes, burdened by fatigue, reluctantly unveiled a world determined to snatch her back from the solace of unconsciousness. Morning's harsh rays penetrated the thin fabric of her tent, casting a feeble glow on the worn canvas walls. A makeshift bed of coarse blankets cradled her frail form, the fibres pressing into her weakened frame.

Fixated on her father's boots shuffling into view, Helena watched as worn leather creaked with each step. Jim Swanson, a kind yet weathered man, bore the imprints of a life defined by hardship and love. His eyes, once vibrant, now clouded with concern, surveyed his daughter's struggle against the grip of sickness.

"Helena," he called out softly, his voice cutting through the oppressive stillness of the tent like a gentle melody. Approaching her with the care of years of fatherly tenderness, he said, "Time to wake up, sweetheart."

As she pushed herself up, the effort revealed the gaunt contours of her face. Sweat clung to her pallid skin, and damp strands of hair clung to her forehead. Trying to muster a smile, it faltered into a weak grimace.

Peering into her father's eyes, she expected the usual surge of fear that waking in this unforgiving world brought. However, today, a strange calm settled over her. Deep down, Helena longed for release, an escape from the ceaseless struggle against an illness determined to claim her.

Jim crouched beside her, a weathered hand brushing a strand of hair from her clammy brow. His touch, a soothing balm, momentarily eased the ache that radiated through Helena's weakened body.

"Helena, how are you feeling?" Jim asked, his voice tinged with worry.

She managed a faint, resigned smile. "Same as always, Dad. Just tired."

His gaze held a mixture of love and sorrow, gently squeezing her hand. "I'll fetch some water and breakfast. We'll get you back on your feet, sweetheart. You'll see."

As Jim rose, Helena watched his retreating figure, her father's silhouette a comforting presence against the harsh backdrop of their makeshift town. The canvas walls whispered in the breeze, and the indifferent world outside hinted at her struggle. Yet, in her father's eyes, a silent promise lingered—to stand by her side until the very end.

The sounds of the makeshift town stirred—the murmur of conversations, clattering pots and pans, distant laughter of children playing. The air carried a peculiar scent, a blend of dust and something metallic, revealing the nature of their world.

The makeshift town, a haven for those surviving in the shadows, bore the scars of an existence teetering on the edge. Tattered tents dotted the landscape, makeshift structures leaned for support. People moved with a quiet urgency, faces marked by the struggle for survival.

As the town bustled, Helena closed her eyes, embracing the fleeting relief death promised. In the hushed tent, the bond between father and daughter stood resilient—a fragile thread woven through the fabric of their shared existence in a world hiding dangers beneath the surface.

As Jim vanished into the bustling makeshift town, Helena's tent stirred with the lively entrance of her best friend, Lucy Sparks. With vibrant blue eyes and a cascade of wild auburn curls, Lucy exuded a magnetic energy that cut through the sombre surroundings like a beacon. Her last name was a curious contradiction to her spirited personality—Lucy Sparks, a radiant light in their dim world.

"Hey, Helena!" Lucy chimed, ducking into the tent with a mischievous grin. "You look like you've been wrestling with a sandstorm. Tough night?"

Helena managed a weak laugh. "More like a dance with the Reaper, Lucy. Same old, same old."

Perching on a makeshift stool, Lucy's gaze held a mix of concern and playful teasing. "Well, you know what they say, darling. If you can laugh in the face of death, you've pretty much conquered it."

Helena mustered a smile. "So what's the latest gossip in town, Lucy Sparks?"

Lucy rolled her eyes dramatically. "Oh, you know, the usual. Surviving in this post-apocalyptic carnival of delights. Town's buzzing like a beehive. I heard Carl found a stash of chocolate. Chocolate, Helena! Can you believe it?"

Helena chuckled, the banter injecting a much-needed dose of levity. "I'd believe it if I tasted it. But we both know that's a luxury I can't afford right now."

Lucy's gaze softened. "Helena, you need a break. A real break. How about tonight we forget about this madness and just enjoy the moment?"

Raising an eyebrow, Helena's exhaustion momentarily gave way to curiosity. "Enjoy the moment? Lucy, we're stuck in a glorified refugee camp, surrounded by God-knows-what, and you want to enjoy the moment?"

Lucy grinned, eyes sparkling with determination. "Exactly! Life is like a twisted carnival, and we're the star attractions. Come on, Helen, muster up the strength for some fun. We'll dance in the face of doom."

Helena sighed, her gaze drifting to the canvas ceiling. "Lucy, my idea of fun is not collapsing from exhaustion every other step. I'm not exactly in the prime of my life, you know."

Lucy leaned forward, her expression earnest. "Helena, you're always fun, even when you're dying. That's what I love about you. Now, promise me you'll at least consider joining the festivities tonight. It might just be the diversion you need."

A playful smirk crossed Helena's lips. "Consider it, Lucy Sparks. But no promises. I might be too busy wrestling with the sandstorm again."

Lucy laughed, the sound echoing in the confines of the tent. "Fair enough, my sandstorm-wrestling friend. But I'll be disappointed if I don't see you there, waltzing with the end of the world."

As Lucy exited the tent, Helena couldn't help but smile. Lucy Sparks, her beacon of light in the darkness, had a way of injecting hope and laughter into the most dire situations. In a world on the brink, their friendship stood as a testament to the resilience of the human spirit, a spark of warmth in a cold and unforgiving reality.

The air inside the tent felt stifling, and Helena's throat screamed for relief, dry and desperate. Attempting to call out for her father, her voice emerged as a feeble rasp, met with silence. Panic took hold as she pushed herself upright, wincing at the ache coursing through her fragile body. The realisation struck—Jim must be out hunting.

Summoning every ounce of strength, Helena gathered the will to exit the tent. The makeshift town, vibrant with energy, seemed distant as she stumbled toward the forest, the world tilting with each unsteady step. Towering trees provided a welcome respite from the harsh sun, casting cool shadows on the forest floor.

At the forest's edge, Helena glimpsed the shimmering lake in the distance. The sound of flowing water beckoned, and with sheer determination, she pressed on. The journey felt interminable, each step a battle against her own frailty.

Finally, at the water's edge, Helena sank to her knees and cupped her hands, bringing the cool liquid to her cracked lips. The relief that washed over her was a fleeting respite from the persistent ache clinging to her bones.

With a deep breath, Helena allowed herself a moment to savour the tranquillity of the lake. Across the water, a deer moved gracefully through the trees. A small smile played on Helena's lips as she found solace in the simplicity of nature.

Suddenly, a loud crash shattered the peaceful scene. Helena turned, her weakened body tensing, and her eyes widened as she saw Lucy Sparks emerging from the trees, a bundle of firewood in her arms.

"Helena!" Lucy called out, a mischievous glint in her eyes. "Fancy meeting you here. Did you leave your cosy tent just to catch another glimpse of me?"

Helena managed a weak chuckle. "You caught me, Lucy. Couldn't resist the allure of Lucy Sparks and the way she wields an axe."

Lucy grinned, setting down the firewood with a theatrical flourish. "Well, you must really like me to have left the comfort of your tent. Or maybe I'm just that convincing."

Helena's eyes sparkled with amusement. "Oh, definitely. Irresistible, really."

Lucy approached, her gaze softening as she took in the sight of Helena by the lake. "You look like you could use a hand. Or, in this case, some water." She pulled out a flask from her bag and scooped up some water from the lake.

"Here," Lucy said, offering the flask to Helena. "Save yourself the trouble of coming back and forth. I've got enough charm to convince the lake to share its water."

Helena accepted the flask with a grateful smile, the flirtatious banter lightening the heaviness that clung to her. "Well, aren't you just the water-wielding magician? Thank you."

Lucy winked playfully. "Anything for you, Helena. Just remember, next time I perform my magic, I expect a front-row seat."

As Lucy walked further into the forest, Helena couldn't help but watch her retreating figure, a warmth spreading through her weakened limbs. In the midst of the struggle for survival, Lucy Sparks was a beacon of laughter and charm, a source of strength in a world that often felt on the brink of collapse.

The distant echoes of Lucy's laughter lingered in the air as Jim Swanson hurried through the forest toward the lake. The knot of worry tightened in his chest as he caught sight of Helena's frail form by the water's edge. With a mix of relief and concern, he quickened his pace until he reached her.

"Hell, Helena!" Jim exclaimed, his voice a blend of anger and relief. "What in the world do you think you're doing out here? You scared the life out of me."

Helena turned her gaze toward him, her eyes reflecting a mix of exhaustion and defiance. "I needed water, Dad. I can't just lie in that tent and waste away."

Jim sighed, his frustration momentarily giving way to the deep well of concern that defined his relationship with his daughter. Without another word, he scooped her up into his arms, her frail form feeling lighter than he remembered.

"I can't believe you left the tent," he scolded gently, his voice carrying the weight of worry. "What if something happened to you out here?"

Helena winced as he picked her up, but a hint of a smile played on her lips. "Dad, I'm fine. Lucy was here. She brought water."

Jim's brow furrowed, and he glanced over his shoulder at the large, red-stained bag he had dropped. Guilt washed over him as he realised the importance of the task he had momentarily abandoned.

"I'm sorry, sweetheart," he murmured, tightening his grip on her. "I shouldn't have left you alone. It's just... after losing your mother and sister, I can't bear the thought of losing you too."

Helena's eyes softened, and she rested her head against his shoulder. "I know, Dad. But I can't just wither away. I need to fight."

Jim's heart ached at the determination in her voice, a trait she undoubtedly inherited from her mother. He continued through the forest, his pace measured and careful.

"I know, Helena," he said, his voice a gentle reassurance. "And I'll be right here fighting with you. But promise me, no more wandering off alone, okay?"

Helena nodded, her gaze fixed on the canvas walls of the makeshift tent that awaited them. As they approached, Jim noticed Lucy Sparks approaching with a grin on her face.

"Looks like you found her," Lucy called out, her eyes flickering with amusement.

Jim sighed, the lines on his face etched with a mixture of exhaustion and love. "Yeah, and she's not making it easy on me. Thinks she can go gallivanting around without a care in the world."

Lucy chuckled. "Well, you can't blame her for wanting a breath of fresh air. Besides, I was here to keep an eye on her. No harm done, right, Helena?"

Helena nodded, her eyes twinkling with gratitude. Jim couldn't help but appreciate the support Lucy offered, a bright presence in their otherwise bleak reality.

With Helena in his arms, Jim stepped into the tent, the canvas walls offering a semblance of privacy in their tumultuous world. Lucy followed, her infectious laughter filling the space.

As Jim gently laid Helena down on the makeshift bed, he couldn't shake the weight of his worries. Yet, in that moment, surrounded by the ones he cared for, he found solace. The red-stained bag lay in the corner, a reminder of the struggles they faced, and the fragile threads that bound them together in an oppressive world where survival meant more than just enduring.

The rhythmic thud of Jim Swanson's knife against the wooden table outside the tent drew Helena's attention. Through the narrow opening, she watched her father skillfully carve the deer meat, the red-stained bag lying discarded on the ground. The scent of fresh meat wafted into the tent, mingling with the earthy aroma of the forest.

Jim's movements were deliberate and practised as he chopped up the deer, a solemn focus etched on his weathered face. He reached into the bag, pulling out a few scarce vegetables and added them to the mix. The meagre selection seemed incongruous with the hearty stew he was attempting to create.

As Helena observed, her father turned, catching her eye through the gap in the tent. A warm smile softened his features, and he announced, "Stew's on the menu tonight, sweetheart. Real feast, considering."

Her eyes lit up with a glimmer of hope. "Can I have it without the meat, Dad?"

Jim laughed, a deep, rumbling sound. "In a world where things want to eat you, you can't not eat meat, Helena. Gotta keep up your strength."

He turned back to his impromptu kitchen, adding portions of the deer meat into a small bowl. Helena sighed but relented, "Fine, just a little."

Jim brought the bowl over to her, the rich aroma filling the tent. As he handed it to her, she swished the contents around the bowl with a halfhearted attempt at mixing the flavours.

"Try it, sweetheart," he urged, his eyes searching for signs of approval.

Helena took a reluctant spoonful, her taste buds reacting with a mix of reluctance and mild surprise. Since falling ill, her appetite had waned, but the stew proved to be more palatable than she expected. She chewed slowly, savouring the warmth and sustenance it offered.

As they ate, Jim attempted small talk, the banter masking his underlying concern for her well-being. "So, have any boys caught your eye lately?"

Helena raised an eyebrow, her amusement evident. "Dad, it's not like there are many moments to catch someone's eye when you're trapped in a tent."

Jim chuckled. "Fair point. Though, maybe there's someone brave enough to face the sandstorms for a chance to talk to you."

Helena's smile faltered as Jim continued, "But watch out for Lucy. She's a rebel, that one. Bad news."

Her father's sudden disdain for Lucy sparked a quiet rebellion within Helena. "Dad, she's just a friend. She cares about me."

Jim's expression darkened as he dismissed Lucy with a wave of his hand. "Friend or not, she's trouble, Helena. You need to be careful."

As Jim delved into the details of his hunt against the deer, recounting how it had been distracted by something at the lake—something Helena vaguely registered as herself—she found herself zoning out. Her nods became mechanical, a rhythmic response to his words. She drifted away from the conversation, her thoughts entangled in the complexities of their strained world.

In the tent, amidst the fragrant aroma of stew and the distant echoes of her father's words, Helena withdrew into a cocoon of detachment. The stew, the forest, the warnings about Lucy—they all merged into a blur, leaving her lost in the fragments of a reality she struggled to fully grasp.

As the sun dipped below the horizon, casting long shadows over the makeshift town, a quiet urgency settled among the camp's inhabitants. Nightfall brought with it a ritual of survival—camouflaging, hiding, and blending into the shadows to evade whatever might prowl in the darkness.

Helena watched from her spot in the tent, a sense of helplessness settling over her like a heavy shroud. Outside, people hurriedly draped tarps and branches over the tents, concealing their temporary homes in a desperate attempt to avoid detection. The camp buzzed with muted activity, a symphony of whispers and hurried footsteps.

She longed to be a part of the communal effort, to contribute to their collective safety, but her frailty left her confined to the tent. A frustration tugged at her heart as she observed the shadows dancing on the canvas walls.

Jim, always vigilant, approached the tent, his face etched with concern. "I hate to leave you alone, sweetheart, but I've got camp watch tonight. It's important to keep everyone safe."

Helena nodded, her eyes reflecting a mixture of fear and understanding. "I know, Dad. But I don't like being alone."

He sat down beside her, tucking the blankets around her with a gentle touch. "I wish I could stay with you, but I need to do this. We all do. It's the only way we survive."

Helena's gaze lingered on her father's weathered face, the lines etched by the hardships of their world. "What if something happens to you out there?"

Jim leaned in, placing a soft kiss on her forehead. "I'll be careful, sweetheart. And besides, we've fortified the camp. It's just a precaution. Everything will be okay."

Helena's eyes welled with unspoken fear, not just for herself but for the man she called Dad, the only family she had left. "Promise me you'll come back, Dad."

Jim smiled, a tender reassurance in his eyes. "I promise, Helena. I'll always come back to you."

As he stood to leave, Helena stared at the tent's entrance, her anxiety building with each passing moment. Jim zipped it shut, leaving her in the hushed confines of their temporary haven. Alone in the dim light, Helena strained her ears to catch the distant sounds of the night—the whispers of the wind, the rustle of leaves, the creaking of the camouflaged structures. The canvas walls seemed to close in, and a silent fear gripped her heart.

Yet, amid the darkness, a flicker of hope remained. Jim's promise lingered in the air, a tether anchoring her to the precarious reality of their existence. She lay there, staring at the tent's ceiling, her thoughts a swirl of anxiety and longing. In the night's silence, she clung to the belief that, somehow, they would endure the shadows and emerge into the dawn of another day.

A soft rustle outside the tent caught Helena's attention, and she turned to see Lucy Sparks slipping through the entrance with a mischievous grin on her face. In her arms, Lucy carried an assortment of fabrics in various colours and patterns, a mix of makeshift glamour in the heart of their unsettling reality.

"Guess what, Helena?" Lucy announced, her eyes sparkling with excitement. "Tonight, we're not just surviving; we're living!"

Helena couldn't help but smile at Lucy's enthusiasm, a welcome diversion from the weight of the night. "Living, huh? What's the occasion?"

Lucy winked. "Well, I figured, why not inject a little glamour into our lives? We might be living in the shadows, but that doesn't mean we can't shine."

As Lucy spread the fabrics across the floor, the girls delved into a world of makeshift fashion. They draped the fabrics over their shoulders, twisted and turned them, experimenting with different styles. Laughter echoed in the tent as they joked about their makeshift runway, the vibrant colours contrasting with the sombre reality outside.

"Now, for the pièce de résistance," Lucy declared, revealing a small bag containing what she called "makeup." The contents were meagre—ashes mixed with water, berries for colour—but in their hands, they became tools of transformation.

Helena hesitated, unfamiliar with the concept of makeup in a world stripped of luxury. "I don't know about this, Lucy. It feels... strange."

Lucy grinned, dipping her fingers into the makeshift concoction. "Trust me, Helena. Tonight, we're not just surviving; we're living."

As Lucy applied the rudimentary makeup, a hesitant smile played on Helena's lips. The electric touch of Lucy's fingertips on her cheek sent a subtle shiver through her, a sensation that felt strangely comforting.

"There you go, a touch of glamour for a special night," Lucy proclaimed, stepping back to admire her handiwork. "Now, for the grand finale."

She took a step forward, cupping Helena's face in her hands. The touch was gentle, yet electric, and Helena couldn't help but feel a warmth spreading from Lucy's fingertips to her very core.

"Ready to light up the night, Helena?" Lucy asked, her eyes locking onto Helena's.

Helena hesitated, her nerves bubbling beneath the surface. "I'm not sure, Lucy. I'm not exactly in the best shape, and the night scares me."

Lucy's expression softened, a mixture of understanding and determination. "Helena, tonight is different. I want to live. And I hope for you to be a part of that."

With Lucy's encouragement, Helena felt a surge of newfound strength. The canvas walls of the tent seemed to expand, allowing a glimpse of the vibrant world outside.

"Okay," Helena said, her voice carrying a newfound resolve. "Let's light up the night, Lucy."

As they stepped out of the tent, draped in makeshift glamour and touched by the essence of survival, the night embraced them with its shadows. In Lucy's company, Helena felt a connection that transcended the harsh realities of their world. The vibrant colours, the makeshift makeup, and the shared laughter were a testament to their defiance against the darkness.

Not just surviving, living. The words echoed in Helena's mind as she stepped into the night, her hand intertwined with Lucy's. In that moment, the camp transformed into a canvas of possibilities, and under the moonlit sky, they dared to embrace the flickering flame of life amidst the shadows.

The woods whispered with the secrets of the night as Lucy guided Helena through the darkened paths, her arm wrapped around Helena's waist for support. The makeshift glamour clung to them, catching the moonlight in sporadic glimmers. The barn loomed ahead, its rustic façade transformed into a haven of flickering candles and makeshift decorations.

As they entered the barn, the lively sounds of laughter and music filled the air. A group of youngsters revealed in the makeshift celebration, their laughter echoing in the cavernous space. Lucy led Helena through the crowd, introducing her to a few familiar faces.

"This is Kai and Mara," Lucy said, gesturing to a couple with weathered faces that told tales of survival. "And this is Zara, and you know Carl."

Helena offered a tentative smile, still adjusting to the newfound camaraderie. The youngsters welcomed her warmly, their eyes carrying stories of resilience and shared struggles.

In a corner of the barn, a makeshift bar had been set up, complete with a few barrels and a collection of makeshift drinkware. Lucy motioned to the group behind the bar, a motley crew of youngsters eager to showcase their brewing skills.

"This is Toren, Luna, and Jax," Lucy introduced, a proud grin on her face. "They're the master brewers tonight."

Toren, with wild hair and a twinkle in his eye, poured a concoction into a cup and handed it to Helena. "Potato beer. It's our specialty. Welcome to the party!"

The makeshift beer, though lacking the refinement of pre-dystopian spirits, carried a warmth that spread through Helena. She sipped it tentatively, the taste surprisingly palatable. As the night unfolded, the barn transformed into a haven of revelry. The makeshift dance floor swayed to the rhythm of laughter and music, the flickering candles casting shadows on the faces of those who dared to embrace the joy of the moment.

Lucy stayed by Helena's side, a silent pillar of support. She noticed Helena's occasional moments of weakness, ensuring not to leave her friend alone for too long. They danced under the moonlit sky, their movements a blend of energy and surrender. Helena, despite her frailty, tapped into a wellspring of determination, determined to be part of this night of living. The barn echoed with the thud of makeshift music, laughter, and the rhythmic dance of the revellers. Lucy, ever watchful, shared smiles and whispered words of encouragement, the connection between them deepening with each shared moment.

As the night wove its tapestry of memories, Helena found herself lost in the dance, the laughter, and the makeshift celebration of life amidst the shadows. In the company of newfound friends and Lucy's unwavering support, she experienced a fleeting taste of normalcy in a world that often felt anything but. Not just surviving, living—those words resonated in the flickering light of the barn, a beacon of hope amidst the darkness that sought to engulf them all.

Amidst the lively revelry in the barn, a new challenge unfolded—a makeshift drinking game that involved standing on a stool with one foot while attempting to chug a drink. Jax and Kai faced off in a competition that had the crowd cheering and laughing. Jax emerged victorious, a triumphant grin on his face as Kai conceded with good-natured camaraderie.

As the laughter subsided, Luna stepped forward, a twinkle in her eye. "I bet I can handle my drink better than anyone here!" Zara and Carl, on cue, began chanting, "Helena! Helena! Helena!"

The spotlight shifted to Helena, her cheeks flushing with both embarrassment and anticipation. Mara, sensing her hesitation, offered a reassuring smile. "Come on, newbie! Show them what you're made of."

Lucy, ever attentive to Helena's well-being, spoke up. "You don't have to, Helena. It's all in good fun."

But Helena, fueled by the spirit of the night, replied with a determined glint in her eyes, "No, I want to. Tonight is about not just surviving, but living."

With cheers from the crowd, Helena stepped up onto the stool, balancing on one foot with a cup in her hand. Toren filled it with the homemade brew, and the challenge began.

The first round passed without a hitch, Helena's resolve evident in her steady balance and measured sips. The crowd erupted in cheers, and even Lucy couldn't help but smile at her friend's tenacity.

The second round followed suit, the atmosphere filled with the rhythmic chants of the onlookers. But as Helena took the cup for the third time, a shadow of unease crossed her face. Beads of sweat formed on her forehead, panic flickering in her eyes. The room spun, her chest tightened, and a wave of dizziness overcame her.

Lucy, sensing something was amiss, rushed to Helena's side as she collapsed to the ground. The cheers and laughter faded into the background, replaced by a concerned hush.

"Helena, are you okay?" Lucy asked, kneeling down next to her. Helena, still catching her breath, managed a weak nod. "I'm okay, Lucy. I just... I want to go home."

Lucy nodded in understanding, her concern etched across her face. With gentle assistance, she helped Helena to her feet, supporting her as they made their way through the crowd. The revelry continued around them, but in that moment, Helena's focus was on the makeshift exit and the promise of the familiar safety of their tent.

The night had taken an unexpected turn, a reminder that even in moments of celebration, the fragility of their existence persisted. As Lucy guided Helena through the barn doors, the sounds of laughter and music faded into the night, leaving behind the echoes of a night where the line between survival and living had blurred, if only briefly.

The night air was thick with tension as Lucy and Helena stumbled through the darkened woods, the distant echoes of revelry replaced by an unsettling silence. The atmosphere shifted abruptly when a blood-curdling scream pierced the stillness, sending shivers down their spines.

Without a second thought, they began to run, Helena's unsteady steps matched by Lucy's urgency. However, it didn't take long for Helena's weakened state to betray her, and she stumbled, collapsing to the ground. Fear gripped her as she struggled to rise, but her strength waned.

Lucy, swift and resolute, scooped Helena into her arms, determination etched on her face. With Helena clinging to her, Lucy sprinted through the trees, the scream now replaced by distant, ominous rustling.

As they neared the camp, Lucy's steps quickened. The makeshift tent loomed ahead, a beacon of both refuge and uncertainty. With one swift motion, Lucy carried Helena inside, gently depositing her onto the makeshift bed.

"Stay quiet, Helena," Lucy whispered urgently, her eyes scanning the confines of the tent. She reached for a stake, gripping it tightly in her hand.

Helena, wide-eyed and trembling, clutched at the edges of the makeshift blanket. "What was that scream, Lucy? What's happening?"

Lucy pressed a finger to her lips, signalling for silence. "We don't know, but we need to stay quiet. I won't leave your side."

As Lucy settled beside Helena, her gaze fixed on the tent entrance, Helena's chest tightened with fear. The air inside the tent felt charged with uncertainty, the silence broken only by the distant rustling of leaves.

In the eerie calm, Lucy reached for Helena's hand, their fingers entwining as a gesture of shared strength. The makeshift stake lay between them, a makeshift defence against the unknown.

Helena's breaths were shallow, her eyes darting nervously. Lucy, however, maintained a vigilant watch, her eyes scanning the darkness beyond the canvas walls.

The night hung heavy with anticipation, and as they lay there in the confines of their makeshift haven, Lucy's presence became a source of solace. In the face of the unknown, the strength of their connection forged a fragile sanctuary. The distant sounds of the night seemed to amplify their vulnerability, yet Lucy's determined gaze and unwavering resolve offered a promise of protection.

The night pressed on, and Helena clung to the edges of consciousness, Lucy's grip on the stake never wavering. In the quietude, their breaths became a shared rhythm, a fragile symphony in the darkness. The confines of the tent held the weight of both fear and camaraderie, a testament to the delicate balance between survival and the threadbare semblance of living in their unsettling world.

As the hours stretched into the night, Lucy's reassuring presence in the dimly lit tent became a haven for Helena. Despite the looming uncertainty outside, they found solace in sharing their dreams for a future beyond the harsh realities of their oppressive existence.

Helena hesitated, voicing her uncertain thoughts about the future, her illness casting a shadow over her aspirations. "I don't even know if I'll make it past a few months, Lucy. How can I dream of the future?"

Lucy, unwavering, clasped Helena's hand, a comforting gesture in the darkness. "Helena, you can't let fear dictate your dreams. Things will be okay, I promise."

With that, Lucy began to paint a vivid picture of a farm—a place where her grandparents had worked, a haven that some of her family currently called home, a sanctuary they would visit soon. She spoke of the rolling hills, the vibrant green pastures, and the smell of the earth after a fresh rain.

"On the farm, there's a chicken named Daisy, a pig named Percy, a cow named Buttercup, and a sheep named Charlie. Oh, and there's the sheepdog, Max. He's the friendliest little thing you've ever seen," Lucy described, her voice carrying the warmth of cherished memories.

Helena couldn't help but smile at the imagery Lucy conjured. The thought of a farm with a quaint assortment of animals and a loyal sheepdog sparked a glimmer of hope within her weary heart.

"And the fruits and vegetables!" Lucy continued, her voice animated with excitement. "Rows and rows of tomatoes, cucumbers, apples, and strawberries. You'll have all the fresh produce you could wish for."

Helena's smile deepened at the prospect of a life filled with such simple joys. Lucy, sensing the impact of her words, reached over to brush a strand of hair away from Helena's face, her touch gentle and comforting.

As the night wore on, Lucy's soothing words and the comforting dreams of a future farm wrapped around Helena like a protective cocoon. In the hushed confines of their tent, they talked of dreams, of animals with endearing names, and of a life filled with laughter and fresh produce.

Lucy, with a tenderness that transcended the bleakness of their reality, brushed Helena's hair as she whispered assurances of hope. "Everything is going to be alright, Helena. We're going to live, and we'll live happily."

With those words echoing in the quiet of the night, Helena drifted into a restless sleep, clinging to the promise of a brighter future. The night ended with the fragile hope of dreams, unaware of the challenges that awaited with the dawn.

Chapter Two

The scent of lavender

Helena's eyes fluttered open, and for a moment, she found herself suspended in the hazy realm between dreams and reality. The air was thick with the soothing scent of lavender, and the soft, diffused light bathed the room in a gentle, purple hue. She lay on a plush lavender canopy bed, surrounded by lavender-scented pillows, her fingers grazing against the silky lavender sheets.

As her senses slowly awakened, panic surged through her. This wasn't her tent, and this wasn't the camp. The Lavender Suite—those words echoed in her mind, a distant memory of voices, a dissonant melody in the symphony of her confusion. The room, adorned in various shades of lavender, felt oppressively peaceful. Lavender-patterned wallpaper, lavender drapes framing the locked windows, lavender furniture meticulously arranged—all conspiring to create an illusion of tranquillity. But to Helena, it was a terrifying calm that clung to her like a suffocating embrace.

She attempted to sit up, her movements sluggish, as if the lavender-infused air weighed down on her limbs. Her disorientation intensified as she surveyed the opulent surroundings. Lavender-scented candles flickered on lavender-scented tables, casting dancing shadows that whispered tales of a reality she couldn't grasp.

The door beckoned to her like an elusive escape, and with a jolt of urgency, she swung her legs over the edge of the bed. As her feet touched the lavender carpet, the plushness beneath her soles only deepened the surreal nature of the Lavender Suite.

His hand reached for the doorknob, fingers trembling as she turned it. The door, however, remained steadfast, its resistance sending ripples of panic through her. She tried again, desperation clawing at her throat, but the lock held firm.

She staggered towards the lavender-draped windows, the bolts obscuring any view of the world outside. The peaceful facade of the Lavender Suite now felt like a cage, its intoxicating fragrance a seductive prison that masked the terror beneath.

As the realisation sank in—the Lavender Suite was not a haven, but a gilded trap—an echo of footsteps resonated outside the locked door. Helena's heart pounded in her chest as the air betrayed its facade of serenity. She pressed her ear against the lavender door, trying to discern the approaching presence.

A soft melodic humming reached her ears as panic surged within her. The rhythmic steps drew closer, and a shadow played on the lavender carpet beneath the door.

Helena retreated from the door, her mind racing with questions. Where was she? How did she end up in this Lavender Suite? Who was approaching?

The door creaked open, revealing a woman draped in lavender silk—a vision of elegance that contrasted sharply with Helena's fear. The woman's lavender eyes met Helena's, and a serene smile graced her lips.

"Welcome to the Lavender Suite, dear. I hope you find it as enchanting as I intended," the woman said, her voice a velvet whisper that added to the surreal atmosphere.

Helena, trapped in the lavender-scented room, searched the woman's eyes for answers, but all she found was an unsettling calm that mirrored the Lavender Suite's deceptive tranquillity. As the door swung shut behind the mysterious figure, Helena's sense of entrapment deepened, and the intoxicating lavender air threatened to drown her in its suffocating embrace.

Genevieve's lavender eyes bore into Helena's, and a small, elegant smile played on her lips. The rich scent of lavender enveloped them as Genevieve, draped in flowing lavender silk, extended a graceful hand.

"I am Genevieve, dear," she said, her voice retaining its velvety calm. "Your trainer, if you will."

Helena, still perched on the edge of the lavender canopy bed, eyed Genevieve warily. The mere mention of being a "Blood Bride" sent shivers down her spine, and the Lavender Suite felt more like a gilded cage than ever.

"You're safe now, Helena. The chaos of the outside world cannot touch you here," Genevieve continued, her movements as fluid as the lavender silk that adorned her.

Helena's eyes darted around the Lavender Suite, the opulence only deepening her sense of unease. "Safe?" she repeated, her voice barely above a whisper. "I don't even know where 'here' is. What is this place?"

Genevieve sighed, a measured response to Helena's resistance. "You are in the Nest now, girl. A sanctuary. A place where you can thrive. You need to stop worrying about what you believe in and start looking at what is right in front of you."

The intensity in Genevieve's lavender eyes was almost overbearing, and Helena felt a wave of vulnerability wash over her. The realisation that she was at the mercy of this elegant and enigmatic figure weighed heavily on her already burdened shoulders. Genevieve gilded closer, her lavender-scented aura enveloping Helena. "It's time to accept your reality, Helena. The outside world is a desolate wasteland. The Nest offers safety, luxury, and purpose. You can choose to embrace it or resist, but resistance will only bring you pain."

Helena's fingers tightened around the lavender sheets, her gaze locking with Genevieve's unwavering stare. The Lavender Suite, no longer just a room but a symbol of a choice she had yet to make, seemed to close in around her.

"Now, do you want a tour or not?" Genevieve's question hung in the air, carrying the weight of an ultimatum.

Helena hesitated, her mind a maelstrom of conflicting emotions. The Nest, with its lavender-scented decadence, felt like a mirage she couldn't quite grasp. Reluctantly, she nodded, a silent acknowledgment that her fate, for the moment, rested in the hands of the elegantly imposing Genevieve.

Genevieve led Helena through the expansive corridors of the Nest manor, a grand gothic structure that exuded both elegance and a haunting sense of permanence. The Lavender Suite was but a small part of this sprawling estate, and the grandeur of its other chambers and halls left Helena awestruck and uneasy.

They entered the ballroom, a cavernous space adorned with crystal chandeliers and intricate tapestries. The air hummed with a melancholic melody, played by a pianist in the corner. Several docile brides, like porcelain dolls, swayed to the music in perfect synchrony. Helena's awe was tinged with a growing unease as she observed their silent movements, like figures trapped in a beautifully macabre dance.

Genevieve, sensing Helena's internal struggle, whispered, "The Nest offers beauty and order, dear. A sanctuary for those who embrace it willingly."

They moved through the library, its shelves lined with ancient tomes and forbidden knowledge. The dining hall boasted a grand table set for an opulent feast, but the silence that enveloped the room added a layer of eerie stillness.

As they strolled through the guarded garden, Helena noticed other brides standing in silence, their eyes vacant yet haunted. The manicured rose bushes seemed to conceal the true nature of their captivity.

Genevieve pointed out the private tower chambers, cautioning, "Helena, those chambers are off-limits. You won't need to venture there if you accept the tranquillity of the Nest. Resist, and you may find yourself in places you'd rather avoid."

The grandeur of the manor was intoxicating, but Helena couldn't shake the feeling that every aspect of this place was designed to lull its inhabitants into submission.

Finally, they reached a nondescript door, different from the ornate ones they had passed. Genevieve's lavender eyes locked onto Helena's as she said, "Are you ready to meet him?"

Confusion clouded Helena's expression. "Meet who? What is this place?"

Genevieve's elegance remained unbroken, her demeanour poised. "All will become clear in time, dear. The Nest demands acceptance. Embrace it, and you shall find purpose within its walls."

The door creaked open, revealing a dimly lit chamber beyond. The haunting elegance of the Nest reached a crescendo, and Helena, torn between awe and apprehension, stepped into the unknown, unsure of what awaited her in this mysterious sanctuary.

The door to the dimly lit chamber opened, and Helena found herself face to face with Nikolai, the enigmatic vampire who had chosen her to be a part of the Nest. He stood in the centre of the room, his presence both commanding and disconcertingly youthful.

"Helena," he greeted with a charming smile, his lavender eyes gleaming. "I'm delighted to finally meet you. Please, have a seat."

The opulent dining room was bathed in a soft, golden light. A long table stretched before them, adorned with silverware and crystal glasses. Helena cautiously took a seat, her eyes never leaving Nikolai, who elegantly settled into the chair across from her.

Nikolai tried to charm her with tales of his immortal existence, his eyes sparkling with a youthful exuberance that seemed at odds with his ageless appearance. He spoke of art, literature, and the intricacies of vampire culture. Yet, Helena remained distant, her responses measured and guarded.

As the evening unfolded, Nikolai extended an invitation for her to dine with him every night. "I would be honoured to share this time with you, Helena. You are a fascinating addition to the Nest."

That evening, Helena cautiously attended the lavish dinner. The grandeur of the setting overwhelmed her, and the overbearing presence of Nikolai made it difficult for her to focus on anything else. He sat across from her, his gaze fixated on her every move. The table was adorned with an array of exquisite dishes, but Nikolai made no move to eat. When Helena hesitantly asked if he wasn't hungry, he simply replied, "Later."

Awkwardness hung in the air as Helena tried to navigate the stifling atmosphere. Nikolai, almost childlike in his fascination with her, seemed eager to please, yet his overbearing presence made the interaction uncomfortable.

"I've been eager to meet you for so long, Helena," Nikolai confessed, his lavender eyes fixed on her. "You are a vision of beauty, and I find myself captivated by your every word."

The evening dragged on, Helena barely able to eat under Nikolai's watchful gaze. The awkwardness escalated when he insisted on discussing her likes and dislikes, seemingly desperate to please her. "Is there anything you desire, Helena?" he asked, his eyes earnest. "I want to make your time here as enjoyable as possible."

The formality of the setting, combined with Nikolai's overzealous attempts at charm, left Helena feeling trapped. Yet, beneath his overwhelming demeanour, she sensed a vulnerability that stirred conflicting emotions within her.

As the awkward dinner neared its end, Nikolai, with an air of eagerness, asked, "May I walk you back to your room, Helena?" She hesitated, aware of the necessity to appease him. "Yes, thank you."

The grandeur of the Nest's corridors seemed to close in around them as Nikolai escorted her. In the midst of this overwhelming and opulent environment, Helena couldn't shake the feeling that every step she took was further entwining her fate with the enigmatic vampire who had chosen her.

Nikolai led Helena back to the Lavender Suite, an air of possessiveness surrounding him. The scent of lavender enveloped them as they entered, and the room, once a haven of peace, now seemed to constrict around Helena.

As the door closed behind them, Nikolai's demeanour shifted. His eyes darkened with an intensity that sent shivers down Helena's spine. Before she could react, he moved closer, his hands on her waist, attempting to be passionate in a way that felt invasive.

"Helena," he whispered, his voice low and seductive, "I've waited so long for this moment."

Helena resisted, pushing against him, her heart pounding with fear. "No, Nikolai, please stop."

But Nikolai, fueled by an ancient hunger, overpowered her resistance. He pushed her onto the bed, his strength rendering her attempts futile. Helena's pleas fell on deaf ears as Nikolai, driven by an insatiable desire, fed on her for the first time.

The room, once a sanctuary, became a witness to a violation of Helena's autonomy. As Nikolai finally released her, his eyes betrayed a moment of remorse. "I'm sorry, Helena. I didn't mean to frighten you."

However, the apology did little to ease the profound sense of violation that Helena felt. She lay on the lavender sheets, staring at the ceiling, unable to move from the fear that gripped her. Nikolai, realising the impact of his actions, left her room with a promise of seeing her again. Alone in the Lavender Suite, Helena felt a profound sense of vulnerability. The room that once symbolised peace now carried the weight of an unwelcome encounter, and she struggled to reconcile the violation with the haunting aroma of lavender that lingered in the air.

The Lavender Suite bathed in the morning sunlight, a stark contrast to the turmoil within Helena. Sleep had eluded her throughout the night, haunted by the echoes of Nikolai's violation. As the sun streamed through her window, she felt the weight of a sleepless night settle into the shadows beneath her eyes.

In the hall outside, Genevieve's voice called out, breaking the uneasy silence. "Lesson is starting, ladies. Move quickly!"

Helena, still clad in the elegant attire from the night before, reluctantly rose from her lavender-draped bed. She joined the procession of Brides making their way to the training area. The hallway, once an opulent passageway, now felt like a corridor of secrets and suppressed rebellion.

Genevieve, standing at the forefront of the group, exuded an intense elegance that bordered on the overpowering. "Welcome, ladies. Today, we commence combat training. It is your duty to protect your vampire, to lay down your life if need be."

Helena's internal struggle intensified. She had been thrust into a world of darkness, her autonomy stripped away. But amid the fear, a spark of defiance ignited within her.

The training ground, once a manicured garden, now served as the arena for a different kind of cultivation. Genevieve, sensing the dormant strength within Helena, selected her for archery training. Helena, physically weakened by her illness, initially struggled to draw the bow. Genevieve's commanding voice echoed across the courtyard, urging her on. "You must do this. Your vampire's life may depend on it."

Fueled by a determination to resist, Helena gritted her teeth, her frail form contorting with the effort. She let out an agonising scream as the arrow finally left the bow, pain rippling through her weakened body. The courtyard fell into a momentary hush, the collective breaths of the Brides suspended in the air.

Genevieve, ever the unyielding trainer, did not relent. "Again! Your vampire needs to know you can protect him."

Helena, caught between pain and the desire to reclaim some semblance of control, drew the bow once more. The struggle persisted, each release of the arrow accompanied by a chorus of pain. Yet, with each shot, a flicker of defiance grew within her.

In that courtyard, amid the oppressive elegance of the Nest, Helena found a surprising talent for archery. The bow became an extension of her resolve, a tool to channel her inner strength. As she shot arrow after arrow, the pain became a testament to her determination, fueling her commitment to continue "not just surviving, living."

The Brides, observing the unexpected prowess, exchanged glances of both admiration and curiosity. Genevieve, her intense elegance undiminished, saw something more in Helena—a defiance that could potentially unravel the carefully woven tapestry of the Nest.

As the sun dipped below the horizon, casting long shadows within the Nest, Genevieve led the group of Brides into the grand ballroom. The opulence of the space overwhelmed them—the sparkling chandeliers, intricately designed ceiling, and polished marble floors exuded a haunting beauty that masked the true nature of their captivity.

"The vampires will confirm their partners for eternity. If you mess up tonight, they have the right to change their mind. Dress accordingly," Genevieve declared, her words casting a chilling undertone over the preparations for the induction ball.

The Brides exchanged uneasy glances as Genevieve summoned attendants to assist in their preparations. Powder puffs and brushes materialised, and an array of extravagant dresses unfurled like petals of a sinister flower.

Helena, caught between the allure of the grandeur and the reality of her captivity, felt a surge of conflicted emotions. As they powdered her face and dressed her in an ethereal white gown, the constricting fabric seemed to form wings upon her back, like those of a swan.

Genevieve, her elegant demeanour a facade for the calculated cruelty beneath, approached Helena with a seemingly caring touch. "You, my dear, are a vision of purity. Gentle and timid, just as you should appear. The perfect complement for your vampire."

Helena, gazing at her reflection in the ornate mirror, saw the twisted symbolism in the ensemble. The swan, though appearing delicate, was known for its fierce defence of its territory. A sudden resolve flashed in Helena's eyes—a silent acknowledgment that, despite the appearance of fragility, she, too, harboured the potential for fierce resistance.

As the attendants continued their meticulous work, Helena's mind wrestled with the conflicting emotions. The grand ballroom, adorned with lavish decorations, seemed like a gilded cage. The makeup, the constricting dress—all were just another means of control.

The ensemble, with its deceptive elegance, spoke volumes about the Nest's manipulation. Helena's transformation into a swan-like figure was not just an aesthetic choice; it was a subtle reminder that appearances could be deceiving.

Amid the scent of powder and the rustle of fabric, Helena felt the weight of her captivity settle upon her. The lavish ball, an induction into a lifetime of servitude, loomed ahead. In her eyes, however, glinted the spark of a swan—gentle in appearance but harbouring the strength to be vicious if the need arose. The Nest might have crafted an illusion, but within the layers of silk and powder, Helena harboured a determination to resist, to break free from the ornate chains that bound her to this gilded prison.

The grand ballroom of the Nest was adorned with opulence, the air heavy with the scent of delicate perfumes and the swish of lavish fabrics. The vampires, elegant and otherworldly, moved among the Brides, their eyes assessing and appraising. Helena, dressed in her constricting gown that seemed to form wings upon her back, tried to blend into the grandeur while suppressing the lingering memories of the Lavender Suite.

Nikolai, resplendent in his dark attire, approached Helena with a courtly bow. His charm was undeniable, and for a moment, she found herself captivated by the grace of his movements. The haunting melody of the waltz began, and Nikolai extended a gloved hand.

"Would you care for a dance, my dear Helena?" he asked, a glint of amusement in his eyes.

Helena hesitated, her instincts at odds with the situation. Yet, to avoid drawing attention or incurring his displeasure, she placed her hand in his, allowing herself to be led to the dance floor. The music swirled around them, and Nikolai's skilled steps guided her through the intricate patterns of the dance.

His eyes, hypnotic and intense, held her gaze. It was almost easy to forget the ominous nature of their connection. She must remind herself—he was the enemy. The enchanting atmosphere of the ball threatened to blur the lines between captive and captor.

As they twirled and spun, Helena tried to gauge his demeanour, searching for any signs of the turbulence from the previous night. Nikolai, however, exhibited none of the darkness that had unfolded in the Lavender Suite. He smiled and conversed with other vampires, projecting an air of normalcy.

Yet, just as Helena began to wonder if the Lavender Suite had been a twisted nightmare, a loud crash shattered the illusion. The music screeched to a halt, and the guests turned their heads toward the source of the disturbance.

In the midst of the shattered silence, a vampire's hiss cut through. A broken piece of a valuable artefact lay at Nikolai's feet, the remnants of an ornate vase that had met an untimely end. Nikolai's expression darkened, and his eyes swept the room, searching for the culprit. The tension in the air thickened as the vampires glared at the assembled Brides, their eyes cold and unforgiving.

Helena, caught in the midst of the chaos, felt a shiver run down her spine. The spell of the dance broken, she now faced the harsh reality of the Nest—an intricately woven web of beauty and danger, where the line between celebration and consequences was razor-thin.

The shattered vase lay on the grand ballroom floor, its broken remnants a stark contrast to the elegance that surrounded it. The guests hushed in uneasy anticipation, their eyes fixed on the source of the disruption.

Helena's gaze darted across the room, and there, stumbling through the party, was a dishevelled figure—Ravenna Stark. Her dress clung awkwardly to her, her movements unsteady. A smirk played on her lips as she locked eyes with Helena, and in a flirty tone, she teased, "Well, if it isn't the new beauty in town."

Before Helena could respond, a loud voice boomed through the room, "Ravenna Stark, watch your tongue!" The crowd parted, revealing the imposing figure of Edward, the head vampire of the Nest.

Ravenna, oblivious to the gravity of the situation, sneered and retorted, "Who cares what the old man thinks?" Her words echoed through the room, and a collective gasp swept through the guests.

Edward, frail and ancient-looking with white hair cascading down his shoulders and a long beard, approached with an unsettling elegance. His six-fingered hands, adorned with sharp, elongated nails, belied a hidden menace. The air around him seemed to carry the scent of death, a pungent reminder of his true nature.

Helena caught a whiff of that morbid odour as he walked past her. It sent shivers down her spine, and she realised that despite his frail appearance, Edward was a force to be reckoned with.

Without a word, Edward's response was swift and brutal. In an instant, he seized Ravenna by the throat, lifting her off her feet. The ballroom fell into stunned silence as he made an example of her, a warning etched in the violent display of power.

Ravenna, gasping for breath, struggled against his grip. Her defiant eyes met Helena's for a fleeting moment, a mixture of resignation and rebellion. The room, once filled with the melody of the waltz, now echoed with the sounds of Ravenna's choked sobs.

Edward's wrath was unrelenting, a dark cloud casting a pall over the celebratory atmosphere. The guests, both vampires and Brides alike, stood frozen, their eyes fixed on the unfolding spectacle. As the violence played out before her, Helena felt a chill crawl down her spine. The Nest, with its grandeur and secrets, had revealed a glimpse of its true nature—a place where defiance carried a heavy price, and survival demanded silent submission. The night ended with the echoes of Ravenna's pain reverberating through the ballroom, a haunting reminder of the perilous dance within the Nest, where each step held the potential for tragedy.

Chapter Three

Dining with dead men

The grand courtyard of the Nest manor sprawled before Helena, bathed in the soft glow of sunlight filtering through ancient trees. Her footsteps echoed against the polished marble as she made her way to the dining hall for lunch. Amidst the opulent surroundings, the illusion of tranquillity clung to the air.

As she approached the secluded garden area, the distant murmur of crying reached Helena's ears. Intrigued and concerned, she followed the sorrowful melody until she discovered Liliana Snow, another Bride, seated on a stone bench. Liliana's frail form shivered with sobs, her eyes red and swollen.

"Are you okay?" Helena asked, a genuine concern etched across her face. She took a tentative step closer to Liliana, who seemed startled by her presence.

Liliana looked up, her gaze filled with a mixture of sadness and foreboding. "You'll find out soon enough," she whispered ominously, her voice barely audible over the rustle of leaves.

Helena furrowed her brow, puzzled by the cryptic response. "Find out what? What's wrong?"

Liliana hesitated, her tear-filled eyes flickering with fear. "Just... don't anger them. It ends badly if you do. Believe me."

A chill ran down Helena's spine as she absorbed Liliana's warning. The air in the secluded garden felt heavy with an unspoken darkness, leaving Helena with more questions than answers.

"I don't understand. What do you mean?" Helena pressed, her curiosity battling with the uneasy feeling settling within her.

Liliana shook her head, unable or unwilling to provide further details. "It's better not to know. Just be careful, or you'll end up like me."

Helena hesitated, torn between a desire to uncover the truth and the pressing need to attend lunch. Reluctantly, she left Liliana's side, the weight of the ominous encounter lingering as she retraced her steps toward the dining hall.

As she walked away, the haunting sound of Liliana's quiet sobs faded into the background. The manor courtyard, with its grandeur and secrets, concealed layers of darkness beneath its polished façade. Helena couldn't shake the feeling that, like Liliana, she had just brushed against the edge of a concealed abyss—one that threatened to engulf her if she dared to defy its silent rules.

The grand dining hall of the Nest manor extended before Helena as she arrived for the meal. A long, ornate table was adorned with an array of lavish dishes, but the atmosphere held an air of tension beneath its veneer of opulence. As Helena approached her designated seat, Nikolai, her betrothed, courteously pulled out the chair for her.

"Please, have a seat, my dear," Nikolai urged, his eyes gleaming with an unsettling intensity. Helena hesitated for a moment before lowering herself into the plush chair.

As the meal began, a disconcerting contrast unfolded. The vampires indulged in conversation and exquisite dishes while the Brides, like captives on display, participated in the illusion of normalcy. Unnerved, Helena observed the interactions around her.

To her left, Serena Springwell, another Blood Bride, chatted animatedly with the vampires, her demeanour unusually cheerful. Serena seemed unfazed by their shared predicament, her laughter ringing through the hall like a discordant melody.

"So, Edward, have you heard the latest gossip from the human world? It's positively scandalous!" Serena exclaimed, her eyes sparkling with an almost manic delight.

Edward, the head vampire, regarded her with a detached interest. "Pray tell, Serena, what intriguing tales have you unearthed?"

Helena, sitting adjacent to Nikolai, couldn't help but feel an unsettling dissonance between Serena's cheerfulness and the grim reality of their captivity. Serena, however, appeared to revel in the role of entertainer, her vivacious energy cutting through the sombre air.

Nikolai leaned in, his gaze locked onto Helena. "She's an interesting one, isn't she? Serena brings a certain... vibrancy to our existence."

As Helena tried to comprehend Serena's seemingly carefree demeanour, a sudden patter of footsteps caught her attention. She turned quickly, her eyes widening at the sight of Serena approaching with an exuberant smile.

"Hello there! You must be Helena Swanson, the newest addition to our charming family," Serena declared with theatrical flair. "I'm Serena Springwell, your guide to surviving—or perhaps thriving—in this peculiar abode."

Helena, taken aback by Serena's grand entrance, managed a cautious smile. The overly cheerful Blood Bride seemed like a burst of colour in a world draped in shadows, and Helena couldn't shake the feeling that there was more to Serena than her outward exuberance suggested.

As Serena continued her lively chatter, Helena's attention wavered. The patterning of footsteps had grown more distinct, and Helena couldn't help but be drawn to the peculiar sight behind Serena. In the hallway, a strange pale girl stood, her eyes fixed on the Brides' training session.

Curiosity overcoming her, Helena discreetly peered around Serena to catch a better glimpse of the enigmatic observer. The girl seemed otherworldly, her appearance almost ethereal. Despite the lively atmosphere of the grand dining hall, the pale girl remained silent, a ghostly figure against the backdrop of the manor.

Unable to contain her intrigue, Helena leaned slightly, attempting to catch the girl's eye. The pale girl, however, maintained her silence, disappearing into the shadows as quickly as she had appeared.

Helena turned to Nikolai, who sat beside her, and asked, "Who is that girl? Why is she watching us?"

Nikolai, surprisingly nonchalant, dismissed Helena's concern with a casual wave of his hand. "Ignore her, my dear. Some residents prefer to keep to the shadows. It's of no consequence."

The dismissal only fueled Helena's curiosity, but before she could press further, Genevieve's commanding voice echoed through the hall.

"Ladies, finish up your lunch. Training will commence shortly," Genevieve declared with a sense of authority. Her words were met with approval from Edward, who grinned in Helena's direction.

"You know, Genevieve, I've always been drawn to a woman in power," Edward remarked, his gaze lingering on Genevieve. He rose from his seat, his movements graceful and almost predatory, and approached Genevieve, kissing her hand with a flirtatious air. Helena couldn't help but wonder about the dynamics between the two. As Genevieve, seemingly accustomed to Edward's advances, maintained her composure, Helena felt a shiver run down her spine. The manor, with its labyrinth of secrets and unsettling elegance, seemed to unfold with every passing moment, and Helena realised that survival in this world required more than just physical strength. It demanded a keen understanding of the intricate dance between power and submission.

As combat training resumed in the grand courtyard, Helena found herself once again standing among the Brides, bow in hand. The rhythmic thud of arrows hitting their targets reverberated through the air as Genevieve barked commands, her piercing gaze evaluating each Bride's performance.

Helena's proficiency with the bow had grown, and with each arrow she released, she approached the bullseye with remarkable accuracy. The courtyard bore witness to her steady progress, arrows hitting the outer rings with precision. On the final shot, determination ignited in her eyes as she aimed for the coveted bullseye.

With a focused breath, Helena released the arrow. It soared through the air, finding its mark dead centre in the bullseye. A surge of excitement overcame her, and against her usual reserved nature, she let out an involuntary squeal of triumph.

Immediately realising her lapse in composure, Helena stifled her excitement, cheeks flushing with a mix of embarrassment and exhilaration. The courtyard fell silent for a moment, the other Brides casting curious glances in her direction.

Genevieve, however, approached with a subtle smile playing on her lips. "Impressive, Helena," she commended, acknowledging the accomplishment. "It seems the swan proves to be fiercely protective of its territory after all."

Helena's eyes widened at the unexpected praise. The mention of the swan, the symbolism of her earlier dress, lingered in her mind. It was as if Genevieve had unravelled a layer of her identity, revealing the hidden strength within.

Determined to harness this newfound strength, Helena's focus shifted. Ignoring the aches in her body, she continued to shoot arrows tirelessly, the courtyard echoing with the thud of arrows hitting targets. The pain was secondary to the burning desire within her—a desire to not just survive but to thrive in this perilous world.

Hours passed, and the sun began its descent, casting long shadows across the courtyard. Helena's hands trembled from exhaustion, yet she persisted. With each arrow, she affirmed her resilience, a quiet rebellion against the confines of the Nest.

As the last rays of sunlight disappeared, Helena stood alone in the darkened courtyard, surrounded by the remnants of her relentless pursuit of strength. The moonlit night bore witness to the silent determination that had taken root within her—an unyielding force against the oppressive elegance of the Nest.

As Helena entered the lavishly adorned dining room, her eyes scanned the opulent surroundings. The grandeur of the Nest was a stark contrast to the haunting scenes she had witnessed in Liliana's grief-stricken eyes earlier. Trying to maintain a semblance of normalcy, she took her seat next to Nikolai, who greeted her with a charming smile.

"Helena, my dear, you look ravishing tonight," Nikolai complimented, his eyes fixated on her.

"Thank you," she replied, mustering a polite smile, though her thoughts remained tethered to Liliana, who entered the dining hall with a heavyhearted reluctance.

As the Brides took their places, the head vampire, Edward, appeared with an air of regality. His pale hands, adorned with six fingers, gripped the edge of the table as he scanned the room with piercing eyes. A commanding presence, he surveyed each Bride with a discerning gaze.

"Ladies," Edward's voice resonated through the hall, "dinner is served. Consume your meals with the grace befitting your stature."

Helena observed the array of decadent dishes presented before them. However, her attention was diverted to Liliana, who sat with vacant eyes, refusing to partake in the elaborate feast.

"Helena," Nikolai's voice interrupted her thoughts. "Join me in relishing this exquisite meal. It's a rare indulgence."

She nodded, turning her focus to her plate, but her concern for Liliana lingered.

Meanwhile, Edward's patience wore thin with Liliana's resistance. "Liliana, my dear, you must eat. Starving yourself will only lead to despair."

Liliana's gaze remained distant, her refusal to eat an emblem of her internal struggle. The Brides watched in tense silence as Edward's tone grew stern.

"Enough of this defiance," he declared, his six-fingered hand reaching out to grasp Liliana's arm with an unsettling force.

A cry escaped Liliana's lips as Edward forcibly pulled her from her seat, dragging her out of the dining room. Her screams echoed down the hallway, leaving the remaining Brides frozen in a mixture of fear and helplessness.

Helena's heart raced as she watched the disturbing spectacle unfold. The stark reality of their captivity weighed heavily on her, and a growing determination to resist this oppression kindled within her. In the chilling silence that followed, the Brides exchanged uneasy glances, their shared plight etched in their haunted eyes.

Etiquette lessons in the grandiose Nest manor were a surreal affair. The Brides, each adorned in their lavishly elegant dresses, gathered in the refined chamber under the watchful eye of Genevieve. The air was heavy with the scent of intrigue and tension, the weight of the vampires' expectations looming overhead.

As Genevieve began imparting the nuances of etiquette, Ravenna Stark couldn't resist the urge to interject with her characteristic sarcasm. Her comments were like rebellious sparks in the stifling atmosphere, challenging the expectations placed upon them.

"Well, aren't we the epitome of refinement," Ravenna drawled, her tone dripping with mockery. "I do believe I'm ready for the royal court now."

Genevieve's eyes narrowed, her patience tested by Ravenna's audacity. "Ravenna, etiquette is a crucial aspect of our existence here. It ensures the smooth functioning of the Nest."

Ravenna smirked, undeterred. "Smooth functioning? How quaint. I'd rather be a bit rough around the edges."

Helena couldn't help but stifle a quiet laugh, her amusement mirrored by a few other Brides who shared glances of camaraderie. In this sea of controlled formality, Ravenna's boldness was a breath of rebellious air.

Genevieve's control, however, remained steadfast. She addressed Ravenna with a stern gaze, her words measured yet charged. "So impulsive, so spontaneous, you might just combust."

The room fell into a hushed silence as Genevieve's proclamation hung in the air. Despite the tension, there was a shared understanding among the Brides. Ravenna's fiery spirit, while disruptive, provided a momentary escape from the stifling norms imposed upon them.

As the lesson concluded for a break, the Brides dispersed with fleeting glances exchanged between Helena and Ravenna. In the unspoken language of rebellion, a bond began to form—a silent acknowledgment that, in the face of their captors, a spark of defiance could be found in the most unexpected places.

The dimly lit corridors of the Nest manor echoed with a haunting stillness as Helena made her way back to her lavender-clad haven. The air felt heavy with the weight of secrets, and the hushed whispers of the night seemed to weave an enigmatic tapestry.

As she turned a corner, Helena's eyes caught a fleeting glimpse of movement—a figure gliding through the shadows like a ghost. Intrigued, she quickened her pace, her footsteps muffled against the rich carpeting beneath.

The elusive figure continued to drift further down the hall, its form barely discernible. Helena's curiosity overcame her, and she called out, "Wait! Who are you?"

The figure, seemingly undeterred, increased its pace, the edges of its silhouette flickering like mist. Helena ran after it, her voice echoing through the silent halls. "Stop! I just want to talk. Please!"

At last, the figure halted, its ethereal presence lingering at the edge of Helena's perception. She approached cautiously, sensing an otherworldly aura enveloping the enigmatic form. The shadows seemed to dance around her, distorting reality in a surreal ballet. "I'm Helena," she ventured, her voice echoing in the quiet space. "Who are you?"

The figure turned, revealing a face veiled in shadows, eyes that held a depth of mystery. "I am Violet," she whispered, her voice a gentle breeze that brushed against Helena's senses.

"You're very pretty," Violet remarked, her words carrying a strange weight as if laden with unspoken secrets. "I hope you live longer than my last friend did."

Before Helena could unravel the cryptic message, Violet faded back into the shadows, leaving behind a lingering sense of the uncanny. The corridor returned to an eerie stillness, and Helena found herself standing alone, questioning whether the encounter had been real or a spectral illusion dancing at the edges of her consciousness.

The atmosphere in the training room shifted as Genevieve introduced the next lesson—extracting and storing their blood in vials. The metallic tang of apprehension hung in the air as the Brides gathered around the demonstration table.

Serena, with a smile as bright as the sun, executed the procedure effortlessly. Her movements were precise, her expression composed. In contrast, Liliana, already on edge, began to tremble. As Genevieve explained the importance of mastering the technique, Helena fumbled with the vial in her hands. The small glass container slipped, threatening to shatter on the floor. She watched in awe as Serena flawlessly filled her vial, a serene grace in the way she handled the task.

Liliana's anxiety escalated until it reached a breaking point. Her hands shook uncontrollably, and tears welled up in her eyes. Without warning, she collapsed to the floor, her sobs echoing in the room.

Helena rushed to her side, crouching down to offer comfort. "Liliana, it's okay. We're in this together. We'll survive, I promise." As she spoke soothing words, a sudden, authoritative shortcut through the air. "Such a blubbering Bride, ungrateful wench!"

The source of the commanding voice was unmistakable—Edward, the head vampire.

Liliana, trembling, looked up, and Edward's eyes bore into her with a sinister satisfaction. "Go to my quarters now. I will deal with you later. I need to talk to my Blood Brides first."

Reluctantly, Liliana rose from the floor, her eyes cast downward as she walked toward the dark corridor leading to Edward's cellar. The ominous grin on his face hinted at a sinister pleasure in the control he exerted over the Blood Brides.

Edward turned his attention to the remaining Brides, his gaze lingering on each with an unsettling hunger. The training room, once a haven for shared struggles, now pulsed with a palpable sense of dread, as the Brides awaited whatever twisted revelation Edward had in store for them.

The air in the room thickened with tension as Edward, his grin widening, made a grand announcement. "Ladies, I've decided to grace you all with a gift in celebration of Nikolai's upcoming birthday. Each of you will receive an ornate dress to wear at the grand celebration at the end of the week."

Helena's heart sank as maids entered the room, carrying dresses fit for royalty. The grandeur of the occasion was not lost on some of the Brides, who whispered excitedly among themselves. However, Helena's thoughts were consumed by worry for Liliana, who had been forcefully taken away just moments ago.

As the maids began distributing the dresses, Helena couldn't shake the sense of foreboding that gripped her. The luxurious fabrics and intricate designs seemed incongruent with their captive reality. Helena's concern for Liliana deepened, a silent plea for her well-being echoing in her thoughts.

Reality crashed back down on Helena when Edward, eyes fixed on her, stated, "You must begin planning how you will treat Nikolai on his special day, Helena! He's going to be expecting everything." The weight of those words hung in the air, and Helena's mind raced with the implications. The impending birthday celebration was not just a lavish event; it was a reminder of the sacrifices expected of the Blood Brides. Dread settled over her as she contemplated the loss of dignity that awaited her that night.

As the other Brides chattered about their dresses and the upcoming celebration, Helena's eyes met Liliana's from across the room. In that shared glance, they communicated a silent understanding of the challenges ahead. The ornate dresses, a symbol of forced celebration, were a stark contrast to the grim reality of their existence in the Nest. The chapter concluded with Helena's heart heavy, bracing for the inevitable ordeal that loomed on the horizon.

Chapter Four

When the snow falls

The morning sun cast a pale glow through the curtained windows of the classroom, illuminating the neatly arranged desks. As the Brides settled into their seats for the day's lessons, Helena's gaze instinctively searched for Liliana. Anxiety clawed at her chest when she realised Liliana's usual seat remained conspicuously empty.

Unease etched across her face, Helena raised her hand tentatively. "Genevieve, Liliana isn't here today. Should we wait for her?" Genevieve, typically composed, furrowed her brow at the mention of Liliana's absence. "No, proceed with the lesson. She might have fallen ill or been called away for a moment. We'll check on her later."

Helena couldn't shake the disquiet that settled within her. The morning lesson, a mundane exploration of etiquette and formalities, continued around her. As Genevieve guided the

Brides through the intricacies of cutlery placement, Helena's mind remained preoccupied with thoughts of Liliana.

When the lesson reached its midpoint, Helena mustered the courage to bring up Liliana's absence again. "Genevieve, I'm really worried about Liliana. Can I go check on her?"

Genevieve's usual poise faltered, replaced by genuine concern. "Yes, go. We'll take a break for now."

As Helena rushed out of the classroom, the Brides exchanged indifferent glances. Their chatter filled the room as they dispersed for the break, oblivious to the concern etched on Helena's face. The halls echoed with casual conversation, masking the underlying tension that gripped Helena's heart. Slowly and gingerly, she navigated the maze of hallways, her steps echoing the silent worry that resonated within her.

As Helena navigated the dimly lit hallways, the echo of her footsteps seemed to reverberate with the unsettling worry that had taken root in her heart. The news of Liliana's absence gnawed at her, and her steps carried a sense of urgency.

Suddenly, a soft voice interrupted her thoughts. "Helena."

Startled, Helena turned to find Violet standing in the shadows, her figure almost translucent in the dim light. Violet's eyes, usually distant, bore an unusual intensity.

"Violet, do you know where Liliana is? I'm really worried about her," Helena pleaded.

Violet hesitated for a moment, her gaze flickering as if caught in a struggle. Finally, she spoke, her voice tinged with an ethereal quality. "I saw someone last night. Vladimir. He was hurting Liliana."

Helena's eyes widened with shock and concern. "Vladimir? Who is he? Where did this happen? Is Liliana okay?"

But before Helena could extract more information, Violet's demeanour shifted abruptly. Her eyes darted nervously, and she took a step back. "I have to go now. Be careful, Helena."

Confused and anxious, Helena reached out, "Wait, Violet, please! Tell me more about Vladimir and Liliana. I need to know."

But Violet, with an almost spectral speed, darted away, disappearing into the shadows of the hallway. Helena stood there, a swirl of worry and confusion enveloping her, her mind racing with questions and the unsettling revelation of Liliana's possible predicament.

Helena's frantic knocks on Liliana's door echoed through the corridor, growing more desperate with each unanswered plea. The weight of worry clung to her, tightening around her chest. At the other end of the hall, Ravenna noticed the commotion and approached, concern etched on her usually bold features.

"Is everything okay?" Ravenna inquired, her eyes narrowing in response to Helena's distress.

"No, something's wrong. Liliana isn't answering, and I'm afraid..." Helena's voice quivered as she continued to shout Liliana's name, the panic in her tone escalating.

Serena, appearing from around the corner, overheard the commotion. "I have a key to her room if you need to use it," she offered, her typically cheerful demeanour replaced by a sombre understanding.

Without hesitation, Serena led the way to Liliana's door, inserting the key and slowly turning the handle. The room revealed a haunting silence, disrupted only by Helena's frantic breaths.

As they entered, dread hung in the air like a heavy shroud. The en-suite door was ajar, and their eyes widened at the chilling sight that unfolded before them. Liliana lay in the bathtub, wrists stained with blood, a painful testament to the depths of despair she had endured.

"No, no, no," Helena gasped, rushing forward to cradle Liliana's lifeless form. Her eyes welled with tears as she looked up at Serena and Ravenna, who stood frozen in shock.

A guttural scream tore through the room, escaping Helena's throat in a wrenching cry of anguish. The vampires, with their relentless torment, had pushed Liliana Snow to the brink, and now they faced the consequences of their cruelty, etched in the tragedy that unfolded within the cold confines of Liliana's room.

Helena's world collapsed in on itself as she cradled Liliana's lifeless form. Tears streamed down her face, and her heart wailed with the weight of guilt. In her mind, echoes of self-blame reverberated, the haunting question of whether she could have done more. Serena, her usually cheerful disposition replaced by solemn understanding, tried to console Helena, placing a gentle hand on her shoulder. "It's not your fault, Helena. You couldn't have known."

But Helena couldn't be comforted. The tendrils of guilt wrapped around her, suffocating reason and solace. Her gaze remained fixed on Liliana, and a heavy silence enveloped the room.

Suddenly, the door swung open, revealing the imposing figure of Edward. His cold, dead eyes surveyed the scene, registering Liliana's lifeless form, the distressed Helena, and the frozen expressions of Serena and Ravenna.

"What's this?" Edward's voice cut through the air like a chilling wind. "A Bride has decided to make a mess of herself. Well, we can't have that, can we?"

His callous words stung, and Helena's eyes widened with a mix of horror and disbelief. Edward turned his attention to the other Blood Brides, who flooded into the room with an eerie efficiency. They moved with practised motions, cleaning Liliana's lifeless body as if erasing the traces of an inconvenient accident.

Helena, Ravenna, and Serena stood frozen, unable to comprehend the dehumanising spectacle before them. Edward's gaze, dark and foreboding, shifted to the trio.

"Clean this up," he ordered, his tone laced with a chilling indifference. "And remember, none of you speak of this again. It's an inconvenience we'd all rather forget."

The room buzzed with subdued activity as the Brides moved with detached efficiency. Helena, Ravenna, and Serena were left in the aftermath, silenced by the cruel reality of their existence and the tyrannical force that controlled their every move.

In the quiet stillness of the night, the Blood Brides gathered in solemn unity beneath the flickering glow of candlelight. A hidden courtyard served as their clandestine sanctuary, a place where they could mourn the loss of Liliana away from the prying eyes of the vampires. The air was heavy with grief as they clung to each other, seeking solace in shared sorrow.

Helena, her eyes puffy from tears, stood beside Violet. Their shared pain knit their hearts together, and they wept openly, the weight of their grief impossible to bear alone. Serena, with clasped hands and bowed head, offered silent prayers for Liliana's departed soul. Ravenna, true to her impulsive nature, had brought a small flask of alcohol, which she reverently poured onto the makeshift grave as a tribute.

In the dim light, they knelt around the hastily prepared grave, an offering of love and remembrance for their fallen companion. The uneven ground had been softened by their hands, forming a modest resting place for Liliana's broken spirit.

Genevieve, their enigmatic trainer, stepped forward, her presence commanding the attention of the mourning Brides. With a voice that carried both strength and empathy, she spoke words of blessing and remembrance for Liliana Snow.

"Blessed be Liliana, who walked among shadows and found her peace. May her spirit find solace in the embrace of eternity, free from the shackles that bound her."

Helena, Violet, Serena, and Ravenna listened in solemn silence, their grief woven into the words of Genevieve's tribute. As the words lingered in the night air, each Bride contributed a personal touch to the makeshift grave.

Helena delicately placed a flower, its petals tender and fragile, symbolising the fleeting nature of Liliana's life. Violet, with aching sadness, whispered words of farewell that only Liliana's ethereal ears could hear. Serena, guided by a poetic heart, left behind a handwritten verse, an offering of beauty amidst the sorrow. Ravenna, fueled by her own unique brand of reverence, poured the alcohol as both a tribute and a release.

Together, they stood in the quiet aftermath, the glow of candles illuminating tear-streaked faces. The air was heavy with a shared understanding of the fragility of their existence. In that sacred space, they found strength in unity, a collective resolve to honour Liliana's memory and defy the darkness that sought to consume them.

As they lingered by the makeshift grave, the night whispered secrets of grief and resilience, binding them together in a clandestine sisterhood. In the shadows, Genevieve's presence remained a silent pillar of support, a guardian overseeing their shared lament. The memory of Liliana Snow lingered in the night air, a poignant reminder of the cost of defiance in the face of vampiric tyranny.

As the Brides stood in mournful silence around Liliana's makeshift grave, the night air thick with sorrow, a sudden disruption shattered the solemnity. The shadows seemed to recoil as the imposing figure of Edward materialised in the dimly lit courtyard. His presence cast an ominous pall over the grieving assembly.

The Blood Brides turned to face him, their expressions a mixture of fear and defiance. Edward's eyes, cold and unyielding, surveyed the scene with a contemptuous sneer. In his hand, he held a chalice filled with crimson liquid, its macabre contents all too familiar.

"What is this pathetic display?" Edward's voice sliced through the stillness, his tone dripping with disdain. The Brides recoiled, their grief-stricken faces turning toward the source of the disturbance. Edward approached Liliana's grave with an unsettling nonchalance, and without a shred of remorse, he spat on the freshly turned soil. The shock reverberated through the assembly, each Bride recoiling at the blatant disrespect shown to their fallen companion.

His eyes swept across the faces of the Brides, lingering on each one with a malevolent gaze. "Tomorrow is Nikolai's birthday celebration," he announced, his voice cutting through the air like a chilling breeze. "No more weeping. You will be expected to celebrate as befits your roles. Any deviation will be met with severe consequences."

The courtyard, once a sanctuary for shared grief, now echoed with the weight of Edward's command. The Brides exchanged uneasy glances, their collective pain overshadowed by the looming threat. With a final, disdainful look at the grave, Edward turned on his heel and vanished into the shadows, leaving the Brides in a haunted silence.

The ominous words lingered, and as the courtyard returned to a hushed stillness, a sense of foreboding settled over the Blood Brides. Tomorrow's celebration loomed like a spectre on the horizon, promising a perilous journey into the heart of their captivity. In the face of impending darkness, the mourning Brides dispersed, their collective resolve tested by the cruel hand of fate. The night held its breath, teetering on the precipice of an unknown fate, as the echoes of Edward's command hung in the air like a sinister omen.

Chapter Five

The Happy Town

Nikolai stood outside the Lavender Suite, his hands hidden behind his back, an eager smile playing on his lips. The air was thick with anticipation as he awaited Helena's response to his unexpected proposition. He had chosen this moment to surprise her, a deviation from the elaborate plans for Nikolai's grand birthday celebration.

As Helena opened the door, her eyes widened in surprise at the sight of Nikolai, a cascade of flowers obscuring his face. He presented the bouquet with a flourish, the vibrant colours contrasting with the muted lavender tones of the Nest.

"Helena," Nikolai's voice resonated with an unusual warmth, "I've arranged something special for us. A little escape from the confines of our Nest. A place I like to call 'Happy Town.' Just for tonight."

Helena hesitated, glancing at the lavishly arranged flowers in his hands. The fragrance overwhelmed her senses, a stark contrast to the sterile air of the Nest. "Happy Town?" she echoed, her curiosity piqued despite her reservations.

Nikolai nodded, his eyes glinting with an intensity that suggested hidden motives. "Yes, a place where we can forget about the constraints of our world, if only for a little while. A private date, just you and me."

His romantic overtures took Helena by surprise. She couldn't shake the feeling that Nikolai was orchestrating this for reasons beyond a simple celebration. Yet, a flicker of determination sparked in her eyes as she considered the potential significance of this opportunity.

"Thank you, Nikolai," Helena replied, her tone gracious as she accepted the bouquet. "I appreciate the chance to step outside the Nest, even if just for a little while. It means a lot."

Nikolai beamed at her response, his excitement palpable. "I knew you'd understand, Helena. This night is for you, my dear. Prepare yourself for a journey to happiness!"

As they ventured beyond the Lavender Suite, Nikolai continued to shower Helena with romantic gestures, each step reinforcing the illusion of a perfect night. Helena, however, remained vigilant, her senses heightened by an innate wariness. As they left the familiar confines of the Nest, she steeled herself for whatever awaited in this mysterious "Happy Town," a place that seemed both enchanting and foreboding in its secrecy.

The air in the Happy Town carried a surreal quality as Helena and Nikolai strolled through its meticulously staged streets. The façade of normalcy was unsettling, the fake shops and homes seemingly frozen in a perpetual day of suburban bliss. Human "Role Players" moved about, acting out their scripted lives with unsettling precision.
Nikolai, revelling in the illusion, gestured toward a quaint bakery where a woman in an apron arranged pastries in a display window. "Isn't it charming, Helena? A slice of life, untouched by our world's complexities. Happy Towns like these allow us vampires to experience a taste of what we've left behind."
Helena forced a smile, her discomfort hidden beneath a veneer of politeness. The inhabitants of this artificial town seemed unaware of the charade, their smiles and gestures practised, devoid of genuine emotion. The concept that these humans were selected to

live out contrived lives for the entertainment of vampires left Helena with a deep sense of unease.

As they continued their stroll, Nikolai pointed out a park where children played with wooden toys, their laughter echoing in the artificial atmosphere. "See, Helena, the innocence of childhood preserved for our enjoyment. Happy Towns are our escape into a world free from the burdens that haunt our existence."

She nodded, her gaze lingering on the faux families and scripted interactions. The realisation that these people were prisoners of a staged reality weighed heavily on Helena. In their efforts to create a semblance of normality, the vampires had ensnared humans in a performance that stripped away authenticity.

Helena glanced at Nikolai, her forced smile fading as her mind grappled with the moral implications of this artificial utopia. Despite the unsettling nature of the Happy Town, a part of her couldn't help but wonder if these people, living within the confines of this staged existence, found a respite that echoed the elusive concept of freedom.

As the night in Happy Town unfolded, Helena navigated the intricacies of this disconcerting facade, aware that her presence was just another layer in the carefully crafted illusion. The staged shops and homes became a backdrop for the dance of a surreal reality—one where vampires, seeking a taste of the normalcy they had lost, revelled in the shadows of borrowed lives.

The flower shop in the Happy Town exuded a vibrant display of colours, the air filled with the sweet fragrance of blossoms. Helena approached the counter, where a woman named "Jenny" arranged flowers with an unchanging smile. There was a vacant look in Jenny's eyes, a lifelessness behind her rehearsed expression.
"Hello there," Jenny chirped, her voice devoid of any genuine enthusiasm. "How may I help you today?"
Helena, sensing something amiss, hesitated for a moment. "Are you okay, Jenny? You seem a bit... distant."
Jenny's vacant gaze flickered for a brief moment, as if an automated response system had glitched. "I'm fine, thank you. Just enjoying another lovely day in Happy Town."
Nikolai, oblivious to the underlying unease, approached with a flourish of romance. "Helena, my love, how about we get you more flowers? A celebration of the beauty that surrounds us."
Helena chuckled, her attempt at levity overshadowed by the disconcerting atmosphere. "You've already overwhelmed me with

flowers, Nikolai. Is there a limit to the beauty you wish to shower upon me?"

A sudden shift darkened Nikolai's expression. "Do you not appreciate the effort I'm putting into making this day special?"

Helena, choosing her words carefully, tried to defuse the tension. "No, Nikolai, it's not that. I just... wasn't expecting so much beauty in one day."

His anger simmered beneath the surface, but he composed himself. "Very well. Let's move on to our next delight, then. Dinner awaits us."

As they walked away from the flower shop, the unsettling encounter with Jenny lingered in Helena's mind. She stole a glance back at the shop, wondering about the lives of the Role Players trapped in this artificial paradise. The facade of Happy Town became more disturbing with each step, and Helena couldn't shake the feeling that the flowers were merely a distraction from the dark reality that loomed beneath the surface.

The fake diner in Happy Town replicated the essence of a typical American eatery, complete with chequered tablecloths and a gleaming chrome countertop. Helena took a seat in one of the booths, a facade of normalcy surrounding her.

Nikolai, seemingly in his element, flashed a charming smile and ordered a variety of dishes. The Role Player waiter, with an eerily rehearsed smile, jotted down the order and left them alone.

As the food arrived, the aroma of burgers, fries, and sizzling steaks filled the air. Helena's appetite, however, was overshadowed by the bizarre charade playing out around her. She eyed the menu, her gaze lingering on the items that held no true sustenance in this fabricated world.

Nikolai, eager to create an illusion of normalcy, encouraged her to try the food. "Come, my dear, indulge in the pleasures of the table. This is your moment to savour the delights of Happy Town."

Helena, despite her reservations, decided to play along. She picked up a fork and knife, attempting to cut into a juicy steak that seemed almost too real. The raw, bloody nature of Nikolai's steak, however, made her stomach churn.

"Ah, the joys of a rare steak," Nikolai exclaimed, savouring each bite with relish. "The taste of life, untamed and unbridled."

Helena forced a polite smile, trying to suppress her disgust. She tentatively took a bite of her own steak, the flavour momentarily distracting her from the fabricated reality. The charade of normalcy threatened to unravel her composure, but she pushed back the discomfort.

In the midst of this surreal feast, surrounded by Role Players engaging in mundane conversations, Helena found herself momentarily drawn into the illusion. The taste of the steak, the ambient chatter, and Nikolai's attempts at charm created a semblance of normal life. For a fleeting moment, she understood the allure of Happy Town—an escape from the bleak existence of the Nest.

As she continued to eat, Helena allowed herself to relax, attempting to find solace in the fabricated joy that surrounded her. Yet, beneath the surface, the unsettling reality lingered, and the taste of the raw, bloody steak remained a stark reminder of the artificial world she found herself trapped in.

Under the artificial glow of street lamps in the Happy Town park, Nikolai and Helena strolled along a winding path. The manufactured tranquillity of the park surrounded them, the scent of plastic flowers attempting to replicate the fragrance of nature. Helena, seizing a moment of relative privacy, decided to broach a topic close to her heart. "Nikolai, have you ever heard of someone named Lucy Sparks?"

Nikolai furrowed his brow, appearing genuinely puzzled. "Lucy Sparks? I'm afraid the name doesn't ring a bell. Why do you ask, my dear?"

A wistful expression crossed Helena's face. "She's... she was my only friend from home. I wonder what happened to her after... everything."

Nikolai, ever the charmer, placed a reassuring hand on her shoulder. "Worry not, my love. It is my birthday wish to bring joy to your heart. I'll do everything in my power to find information about Lucy Sparks for you. Consider it a gift from me to you."

Helena managed a small smile, appreciating his attempt to bring a glimmer of familiarity into her surreal existence. "Thank you, Nikolai. I appreciate it."

As they continued their stroll through the park, Nikolai's eyes subtly caught the fluttering unease in Helena's gaze. He, in his peculiar charm, noticed the shift and addressed her with a soft smile. "My dear, I sense a certain restlessness in those beautiful eyes. Shall we return home? The night is young, and I desire to make the most of my birthday celebration with you."

Helena nodded in agreement, her mind swirling with conflicting emotions. As they headed back towards the fabricated world of Happy Town, she couldn't shake the feeling that beneath Nikolai's charming exterior, there were secrets lurking—secrets that connected the Nest, Happy Town, and the unsettling intricacies of her own fate.

Back within the grandeur of the Nest, the looming presence of Edward awaited Nikolai and Helena. The cavernous halls echoed with the lingering sounds of the birthday celebration that continued without them.

Edward, a vision of regal disdain, intercepted their path. "Nikolai, where have you been? You should be revelling in the festivities, not gallivanting with your Blood Bride."

Nikolai, displaying an uncharacteristic air of nonchalance, waved a dismissive hand. "Edward, my dear, the night is young, and Helena needs her beauty sleep. It wouldn't do for my beloved to look tired on such a special occasion."

Helena, finding Nikolai's defiance amusing, couldn't help but smirk. Nikolai, seemingly unfazed by Edward's disapproval, took Helena by the arm and guided her toward their quarters.

"Rest well, my love," Nikolai whispered to Helena as they parted ways with Edward.

As they retreated into the Lavender Suite, Helena felt a strange mixture of relief and intrigue. Nikolai's rebellious streak offered her a glimmer of hope amidst the oppressive atmosphere of the Nest. Little did she know, the night held more secrets and uncertainties than she could fathom.

The Lavender Suite, bathed in the dim glow of moonlight, seemed to transform into a surreal dreamscape as Nikolai carried Helena across the threshold. The grandeur of the suite was amplified by the gentle flicker of candlelight, casting intricate patterns on the lavender-infused walls. The air was thick with the heady scent of lavender, an intoxicating perfume that masked the underlying tension.

Nikolai's movements were deliberate, his every step echoing with a haunting elegance. He cradled Helena in his arms as though she were a fragile porcelain doll, moving with a grace that contradicted his otherworldly nature. The rich fabric of her gown rustled softly with the movement, and the moonlit room embraced them in a tapestry of shadows and ethereal illumination.

As he gently laid her down on the ornate bed, Nikolai's eyes held an otherworldly intensity. His gaze, filled with an emotion that transcended the boundaries of the supernatural, seemed to lock onto Helena's. The Lavender Suite, with its opulent furnishings and cascading drapes, became the backdrop to an unexpected encounter between a mortal and a vampire.

The room pulsed with an uncanny quiet, and the flickering candles cast dancing shadows on the lavender-scented sheets that enveloped Helena. The atmosphere was charged with an odd sense of intimacy, heightened by the fragrance that seemed to cling to the very air they breathed.

As Nikolai delicately pulled the sheets over her, tucking her in with a tenderness that contradicted his vampiric nature, Helena felt a strange mixture of vulnerability and fascination. It was as if she had stepped into a dark fairytale, where the lines between peril and enchantment blurred with every passing moment.

However, the dreamscape shattered, replaced by an abrupt reality, when a subtle pain on her neck pulled Helena from the illusion. Her eyes fluttered open, and to her horror, Nikolai loomed over her, his lips dangerously close to the delicate skin of her neck. The moment shifted from a romantic tableau to a chilling nightmare. Helena's pulse quickened as she realised the true nature of Nikolai's intentions. The room, once a haven, transformed into a chamber of apprehension and dread.

His fangs grazed her skin, and Helena felt the sharp puncture accompanied by a fleeting sting. The room echoed with the hushed symphony of her own heartbeat, a frantic rhythm that underscored the macabre dance unfolding. The fragrant lavender air became tainted with the metallic scent of blood.

Locked in a gaze with Nikolai, Helena was unable to look away. Her blood flowed into him, a silent exchange that blurred the boundaries between desire and horror. She could see the evidence of her sacrifice staining his lips, the stark contrast between their worlds laid bare.

As the last vestiges of warmth left her body, Nikolai withdrew, a pained expression etched across his features. His fingers brushed gently against her cheek, a remorseful gesture that felt incongruent with the act that had just transpired.

"I'm sorry, my love," he whispered, his voice carrying the weight of regret. "Forgive me. I couldn't resist."

With that, he left the Lavender Suite, the door closing behind him with an ominous finality. The fragrant air, once a sanctuary, now held the echoes of an unspeakable act. Helena lay there, the lavender-scented sheets a poignant reminder of the fragility of her existence. The room, once a dreamscape, now bore witness to the nightmarish reality that lingered in the aftermath of their unholy union.

The Lavender Suite was now a sanctuary tainted, the air heavy with the memory of an encounter that transcended the boundaries of Helena's nightmares. The room seemed to constrict around her, and as she lay on the bed, her fingertips grazed the jagged carving etched into the wooden frame.

The steak knife, a sinister echo from the Happy Town's faux-diner, had become Helena's unlikely tool of rebellion. Gripped in her hand, it became an extension of her defiance, a symbolic gesture to claim a space within the Nest as her own. The blade pressed into the polished wood with a deliberate force, each stroke a declaration of her unwillingness to succumb entirely.

"L.S.," she whispered, the crude initials standing as a testament to a bond that transcended the dark reality of her existence. Lucy Sparks, her anchor to a world that seemed light-years away, existed within those two letters. The carving was uneven, a reflection of the turmoil within Helena's soul, but in its imperfection, it carried a raw authenticity that resonated with her defiance.

As the knife bit into the bed frame, the Lavender Suite, suffused with its aromatic spell, bore witness to a clandestine act of rebellion. The room, with its lavender-draped luxury, held within its walls the subtle manifestation of Helena's strength.

Running her fingers over the crude carving, Helena felt an unexpected sense of solace. It was a minuscule act of defiance, a declaration that even in the face of overwhelming oppression, she could assert some semblance of control over her own destiny. The Lavender Suite, with its regal furnishings and oppressive elegance, became a backdrop for this silent rebellion.

In the quiet of the room, Helena began to speak, her words a whisper carried away by the lavender-scented air. "Lucy, I don't know where you are, but I promise, I will find you. Every night,

I'll look at these letters and remember. Remember that there's a world outside this nightmare, and I'll fight to reach it."

The carved initials, though merely a collection of scars on wood, became a source of strength for Helena. In those moments of solitude, she found herself talking to Lucy as though the carved letters held a connection to her lost friend. It was a ritual born out of desperation, a lifeline to sanity in the midst of darkness.

The Lavender Suite, oblivious to the clandestine conversations and acts of rebellion, stood as both a prison and a canvas for Helena's struggle. In the secret language of defiance, etched into the bed frame, lay the promise of freedom — a promise that, one day, Helena vowed to fulfil.

As the Lavender Suite held the weight of Helena's secret rebellion, the door swung open silently, revealing Genevieve's elegant silhouette. The Blood Bride trainer, with her intense and overbearing elegance, entered the room with an air of authority that demanded attention.

"Helena," Genevieve's voice was a melodic cadence that could both soothe and unsettle, "I thought I would check on you."

Helena, sitting on the bed, looked up, her eyes meeting Genevieve's. The room's lavender hues seemed to shimmer with an ethereal glow as if concealing the untold stories within its walls. Genevieve's gaze fell upon the crude carving on the bed frame. The colour drained from her face, and a subtle tension tightened the corners of her eyes. The atmosphere shifted, a quiet acknowledgment passing between them, words unspoken but understood.

"What is this?" Genevieve's tone was measured, probing. Helena hesitated for a moment, caught between the compulsion to explain and the fear of repercussions. She chose to remain silent. Genevieve sighed, her eyes betraying a hint of concern beneath their composed facade. "Helena, this act of defiance might cost you more than you realise. Promise me, you won't mention Lucy again. It's a dangerous thread you're tugging at."

Helena's shoulders slumped, the weight of an unspoken truth pressing down upon her. She nodded, a tacit agreement that sealed her promise to keep Lucy hidden in the depths of her thoughts.

Alone again, the Lavender Suite transformed into a sanctuary of solitude and secrecy. Helena stared at the initials carved into the bed frame, her fingers tracing the uneven lines. The room, with its lavender-draped opulence, held both her silent rebellion and the silent pain of her compliance.

In the quiet of the Lavender Suite, Helena drew strength from the small act of defiance etched into the wood. The promise to keep Lucy hidden became a solemn vow, a pact made within the confines of her silent prison. As the scent of lavender enveloped her, Helena gathered the fragments of her resolve, finding solace in the knowledge that, even in the darkest corners of her captivity, a small flame of rebellion burned on.

Chapter Six

Wings of Ember

The grandeur of the Nest manor's library embraced Helena as she stepped into its hallowed halls. Dark mahogany shelves reached towards the towering ceiling, laden with leather-bound tomes that seemed to whisper forgotten tales. A distant memory of sunlight filtering through dust motes danced in her mind as she traversed the aisle.

Seeking refuge from the harsh reality that bound her, Helena's gaze fell upon a book with an ornate, gilded cover that seemed to beckon her. Its title, "Wings of Ember," glimmered in golden letters, and the promise of escapism enveloped her like a familiar friend.

As she opened the book, the scent of aged paper wafted into the air, mingling with the faint fragrance of lavender that clung to her. The first few pages cradled an entrancing prologue, weaving tales of an ethereal world where warriors rose against the tyranny of their captors. Helena's eyes widened with anticipation as she delved into the unfolding narrative.

In a realm where shadows cast their veils over lands of despair, a lone figure emerged—a radiant Firebird ablaze with the spirit of freedom. She soared through the skies, gathering a legion of resilient women beneath her wings, each one marked by the scars of captivity and yearning for liberation.

The Firebird's call echoed through the hearts of those who dared to dream beyond their chains, igniting the flames of rebellion. United, they faced the daunting fortress of their oppressors, armed with courage and the unwavering belief that their spirits could not be extinguished.

Helena's fingertips grazed the edges of the pages, her breath caught in the enchantment of the tale. She became lost in the poetic dance of words, momentarily transported to a realm where heroines adorned in armour wielded swords of justice against malevolent forces.

Amidst the chaos, the Firebird stood as a beacon of hope, her wings a tapestry of hues that mirrored the spectrum of freedom. In the moonlit night, she led her sisters with grace and determination, a symbol of resilience that transcended the confines of their once-captive existence.

The allegory resonated with Helena, intertwining with the threads of her own narrative. As the Firebird fought against the chains that bound her people, Helena found solace in the empowering verses. In this tale of liberation, she saw echoes of her own desire to break free from the shackles that imprisoned her within the Nest.

With each turned page, Helena became both the reader and the protagonist, her imagination painting vibrant landscapes where strength and rebellion intertwined. The flickering candlelight in the library cast shadows that danced across the walls, mirroring the dance of liberation she envisioned within the pages of "Wings of Ember."

For a moment, within the sanctuary of the library, Helena was not the captive Blood Bride of Nikolai. She was the Firebird, leading a fantastical army towards the promise of emancipation, her spirit soaring high above the Lavender Suite and the grand gothic manor that sought to confine her.

The creak of the hidden door echoed through the tunnel as Helena, driven by an unexpected sense of curiosity, ventured into the secret depths of the Nest's concealed passages. The air shifted, becoming cooler and carrying with it a subtle scent of aged wood. As she descended further into the unknown, the soft glow of candlelight flickered against the rough-hewn stone walls.

Upon entering the hidden chamber, Helena found herself standing amidst an astonishing revelation—the secret armoury of the Nest. Weapons adorned the walls, gleaming in the ambient light. Swords, daggers, and axes stood alongside rows of polished armour, whispering tales of untold battles. The air held the metallic tang of polished steel, blending with the subtle scent of ancient parchment.

Staring wide-eyed at the unexpected cache of weapons, Helena felt a surge of conflicting emotions. The chamber bore witness to a clandestine world that existed beneath the veneer of elegance within the grand manor. It was a stark contrast to the opulent facade presented to the Blood Brides.

Rows of training dummies lined the room, their straw-filled forms bearing the scars of countless strikes. The dull thud of wooden weapons meeting their targets reverberated, a testament to the covert preparations that occurred in this hidden sanctuary. Helena approached a wooden rack, fingers grazing over the smooth surface of a longbow. Bowstrings hummed like ghostly echoes of the warriors who had once wielded them in the pursuit of skill and strength. The realisation dawned on her—here, beneath the veneer of captivity, the Blood Brides were clandestinely trained for something more than mere submission. A montage of possibilities flashed through Helena's mind, intertwining with the fantastical tale she had immersed herself in just moments before. Perhaps, she mused, the tunnels and chambers concealed beneath the Nest held the promise of a rebellion—a spark waiting to ignite the flames of freedom.

Her gaze lingered on a set of leather armour, intricately adorned with symbols that seemed to speak of defiance. A realisation dawned upon her—the armoury wasn't just a repository of weapons; it was a clandestine haven, a symbol of resistance that transcended the boundaries imposed upon the Blood Brides.

Helena's hands traced the edges of a nearby training blade, the cool touch of metal against her skin resonating with a newfound determination. The secrecy of the armoury unveiled a hidden layer of the Nest—a layer that promised strength, resilience, and the potential for defiance.

As she absorbed the weight of this clandestine discovery, Helena couldn't help but wonder if she could harness the knowledge within the armoury to sculpt her own destiny. The thought of rebellion, once confined to the pages of a fairytale, now seemed to pulse with tangible possibility within the hidden heart of the Nest.

Genevieve's gaze lingered on Helena, studying the shadows that clung to the edges of her eyes, betraying the burden she carried within the Lavender Suite. She extended a hand, the unspoken question hanging in the air, a silent invitation to join the clandestine ranks. The flickering candlelight cast dancing shadows on the armoured walls as Helena hesitated for a breathless moment.

As the two women stood in the heart of the secret armoury, Genevieve, with a regal poise that belied the turmoil within the

Nest, spoke words heavy with purpose. "We're preparing for the uprising, Helena. Training is not a choice but a necessity. Will you stand with us?"

Helena, still grappling with the revelation of this hidden world, met Genevieve's gaze. The offer carried a weight that extended beyond mere physical training—it was an invitation to be a part of something more significant, something that defied the oppressive rules of the Nest. A tentative nod from Helena signalled her silent agreement, and a sense of camaraderie, fueled by the shared secret, enveloped them.

"I believe I can trust you, Helena," Genevieve remarked with a tone that echoed both trust and expectation. "But you must be certain. Can I trust you to keep our secrets, to prepare for the day when we rise against the shadows that bind us?"

Helena, acutely aware of the fragility of her circumstances, felt a flicker of determination stirring within her. "Yes," she replied, her voice unwavering. "You can trust me."

With the unspoken pact sealed, Genevieve gestured towards the array of weapons that adorned the walls of the hidden armoury. "Then let us begin. Survival demands strength, and strength begins with overcoming one's limitations."

Helena hesitated, the tendrils of self-doubt clawing at her resolve. "I am not my strongest, Genevieve. I am sick, weak."

Genevieve's eyes bore into hers, a potent mix of empathy and insistence. "Weakness is a luxury we cannot afford, Helena. Forget the illness, forget the fragility. In this secret realm, you will find the strength within you that transcends the confines of your Lavender Suite. Survival demands it. Can you forget your weakness, if only for the moments we stand together?"

Helena, confronted with the urgent truth of their plight, swallowed the echoes of vulnerability and nodded. "I will forget, for the moments we stand together."

As the promise hung in the air, the secret training began—an initiation into a world where survival meant shedding the veneer of fragility, embracing the strength within, and forging bonds that would withstand the encroaching darkness.

The secret training room echoed with the rhythmic twang of bowstrings as Helena, with precision and grace, sent arrow after arrow flying towards the makeshift targets. Genevieve observed her, a silent guardian overseeing the development of a potential force to be reckoned with.

After a particularly skillful shot, Helena lowered her bow and turned to Genevieve. "I've been practising archery for a long time. I'm already good at it. Can't I learn something else?"

Genevieve regarded her with a discerning gaze, acknowledging Helena's proficiency but recognizing the need for perfection. "You are good, Helena, but the path to greatness demands persistence. With a bow in your hand, you can transcend the ordinary. You can become the greatest. Greatness, my dear, requires mastery. Do not settle for being merely good."

Understanding the gravity of Genevieve's words, Helena nodded, a silent agreement to pursue excellence. She raised the bow once more, focusing on the target with unwavering determination. Each arrow she released spoke of honed skill and unwavering commitment.

As the arrows found their mark, Genevieve approached her with an air of both mentorship and challenge. "You have the potential to be exceptional, Helena. Do not let it go to waste. The bow is an extension of your will, your defiance. Embrace it."

Helena continued her archery practice, pushing the boundaries of her own capabilities, driven by the fervour of newfound purpose. Each arrow embedded itself in the targets with increasing precision, marking the evolution of a once-adept archer into something more.

After a considerable round of archery, Genevieve finally nodded in approval. "Impressive, Helena. Your dedication to perfection will serve you well. Now, let us diversify your skills."

She motioned for Ravenna, who had been quietly observing from a distance, to join them. "Ravenna, come assist Helena. We're moving to the next phase of training."

Ravenna, who had previously been engaged in her own training with Genevieve, eagerly joined Helena, a wicked grin playing on her lips. As Genevieve handed Helena a sleek, silver dagger, she explained, "Helena, it's time to learn the art of close combat. Ravenna will guide you through this."

The clandestine training room transformed into an arena of resilience and empowerment, with the three women—each harbouring their secrets and scars—embarking on a journey that transcended the limitations imposed upon them by the Nest. The echoes of arrows and the clashing of blades against the mannequin targets became a testament to the metamorphosis occurring in the shadows, a rebellion in the making.

The air in the secret training room crackled with anticipation as Ravenna handed Helena a pair of gleaming daggers. "Come at me, Swan. Show me what you've got," Ravenna urged, a glint of challenge in her eyes.

Helena hesitated, uncertainty flickering in her gaze. With a deep breath, she took a step forward, dagger poised. The dance of blades began, Ravenna expertly weaving through Helena's attempts, effortlessly disarming her. Frustration crept into Helena's expression as the knife clattered to the floor.

Ravenna sighed in exasperation, snatching the dagger from the ground. "You've got the aim, Swan, but you need to learn how to use these up close," she remarked, her tone a mix of impatience and amusement. In an abrupt display of skill, she threw the dagger at the wall, the blade embedding itself with a satisfying thud.

Helena's eyes widened at the display. "How did you do that?" she asked, a mix of awe and curiosity in her voice.

Ravenna, initially perplexed by the question, soon connected the dots. "Precision and aim," she mused, a smirk playing on her lips. "You might just be better suited for throwing these."

Intrigued, Ravenna handed Helena the daggers, who hesitated for a moment before gripping them firmly. With a focused gaze, she launched the blades towards the archery targets, each one hitting its mark with astonishing accuracy.

Ravenna arched an eyebrow, assessing Helena anew. "You've surprised me, Swan. Got to admit it, you're making me sweat," she conceded, a hint of admiration in her voice.

As the tension lingered between them, Genevieve's voice cut through the room. "Enough for now, Brides. Take a break and gather your strength. There's more to learn, and we have a long journey ahead."

Helena and Ravenna exchanged a knowing glance, the flirtatious tension dissipating temporarily. The secret training room, witness to their growing skills and the unspoken connection between them, remained a sanctuary of defiance within the oppressive walls of the Nest.

The library's atmosphere was a blend of warmth and tension as Helena, Ravenna, and Genevieve huddled together over cups of tea, seeking solace in shared stories of loss and revenge. The flickering candlelight cast dancing shadows on the pages of the books that lined the shelves.

Helena, her eyes reflecting the haunting memories, began the narrative of her past. "I had a happy childhood," she confessed, a bittersweet smile tugging at her lips. "My mother, my sister, and I lived in a peaceful town. But one fateful night, vampires attacked. They took everything from me—my family, my home."

She paused, a distant look in her eyes, before continuing. "My father and I survived. We lived in a camp for a while. I even had a friend, Lucy Sparks. We were happy for a time, but then... the vampires found us again."

Ravenna listened intently, her eyes reflecting a mix of empathy and fury. "I grew up as an orphan," she shared, her voice carrying the weight of her own tragic past. "One day, vampires invaded the orphanage, selecting us to become their future Blood Brides. I won't let them get away with it. I want to burn down this whole corrupt system."

The bond between them deepened as they shared their stories of anguish, finding solidarity in their shared desire for revenge. As Helena, Ravenna, and Genevieve exchanged tales, a plan began to form in the secret recesses of their minds.

Genevieve, her elegance contrasting with the grit of their conversation, poured tea into delicate cups. "I've been part of the resistance for a long time," she revealed with a sly smile. "Edward may think he's in control, but he's not the puppet master he believes himself to be."

A mischievous glint sparkled in Genevieve's eyes. "I've been secretly poisoning Edward's tea for months," she admitted, a dark laugh escaping her. "It won't kill him, but it does make his beatings less frequent."

Helena and Ravenna exchanged astonished glances, their initial shock giving way to a shared sense of satisfaction. The library echoed with their laughter, an unexpected camaraderie forming among three women bound by a desire for liberation.

As the conversation took a lighter turn, Genevieve, wearing a mysterious smile, leaned in. "I have something exciting for you, Helena. Something that might help us tip the scales in our favour."

Intrigued and filled with newfound hope, Helena's eyes met Genevieve's, and the trio delved into the shadows of the library, forging alliances that transcended the boundaries of their captive existence.

In the dimly lit library, anticipation hung in the air as Genevieve turned her gaze to Ravenna. "Fetch it, Ravenna," she commanded, her tone carrying a blend of authority and excitement.

Ravenna rose from her seat and left the room, only to return moments later with a small, ornate box cradled in her hands. Genevieve, standing tall with a regal grace, gestured for Ravenna to present the box to Helena.

Ravenna gracefully knelt before Helena, offering the box as if she were presenting a sacred relic. However, before Helena could react, Genevieve intervened. "Stand up, Ravenna. This is important business," Genevieve declared, taking the box from Ravenna's hands and turning to Helena.

With a theatrical flourish, Genevieve presented the box to Helena. As she opened it, she revealed a ring—a symbol of rebellion passed down through the resistance for generations. It was a silver band adorned with intricate scrollwork, and a large clear quartz crystal adorned its centre. This crystal possessed ancient magical properties capable of warding off vampires, glowing faintly when they drew near. Engraved inside the band were the words "We live."

Helena's eyes widened as she beheld the ring, recognizing the weight of the legacy it carried. She slipped it onto her finger, feeling its cool metal against her skin. A subtle hum of power coursed through her, a tangible connection to a history of defiance.

Genevieve, with a knowing smile, revealed the secret within the ring. The silver band twisted open, unveiling a small chamber containing powdered wolfsbane—a substance deadly to vampires. Genevieve used her own ring to demonstrate, imparting the knowledge of how to use this potent weapon against their oppressors.

As Helena stared at the ring on her finger, a smile crept across her face. Genevieve's words filled the air, breaking the weight of the past. "Maybe it's the year of the Swan," she remarked, and Helena, a glimmer of hope in her eyes, replied, "Yeah, maybe." In the quiet sanctuary of the library, they stood united by the shared promise encapsulated in the silver band—a promise to resist, to live, and to fight against the shadows that sought to consume them.

The grandeur of the library gave way to the hushed corridors of the Nest as Helena made her way back to the Lavender Suite. The silver ring clung to her finger, a silent emblem of the rebellion she had joined. As she stepped into the room, the scent of lavender enveloped her, a deceptive calm masking the turmoil beneath the surface.

Nikolai awaited her, his eyes ablaze with an intensity that sent shivers down her spine. In a whirlwind of passion, he grabbed her, pulling her onto the bed. Helena's mind raced with conflicting emotions—the power of the rebellion still fresh in her heart, while the proximity to Nikolai demanded a careful dance of deceit.

As Nikolai's hands traced the contours of her body, he couldn't help but notice a change in her, a subtle strength that hadn't been there before. "What's gotten into you, my love?" he inquired, momentarily breaking the feverish embrace.

Helena, quick on her feet, conjured a lie. "Genevieve has been teaching us yoga and meditation," she replied, a deceptive calm in her voice. Nikolai, seemingly satisfied with the explanation, pulled her close once again, drowning any further questions in a cascade of kisses.

The room plunged into darkness, the only illumination coming from the ethereal glow of the quartz crystal on Helena's ring. As Nikolai fed on her, Helena summoned every ounce of strength she possessed, focusing solely on survival. The pain, both physical and emotional, threatened to consume her, but she blanked it out—a warrior in the shadows, biding her time for the rebellion that simmered beneath the Lavender Suite's facade.

Chapter Seven

Once a warrior

Helena's fingers expertly handled the bowstring, and the twang of the arrow echoed in the quiet chamber of the hidden armoury. The rhythmic repetition of her archery practice had become both a physical exercise and a mental escape. As she focused on hitting the bullseye, she felt a sense of purpose, a fleeting respite from the suffocating atmosphere of the Nest. In the midst of her routine, the soft rustle of fabric caught Helena's attention. Her eyes darted toward the shadows, and there, standing hesitantly, was Violet—like a ghost emerging from the dim corners of the secret chamber. Panic gripped Helena's chest, the instinct to run urging her feet to flee from this unexpected intruder.

Yet, something in Violet's demeanour sparked a flicker of curiosity within Helena. Instead of bolting, she shouted for Violet to stop and approached cautiously. In a corner of the hidden room, the two young women found themselves surrounded by weapons and secrets.

"What do you want?" Violet's voice trembled, her eyes darting nervously around the room.

"I want to talk," Helena asserted, her tone a mix of determination and curiosity. "How did you get here? How do you know about this place?"

Violet hesitated before sighing, as if surrendering to an inevitable truth. "I've been sneaking about the Nest for years. I've known about this armoury for a long time." Shadows danced across her face, concealing the secrets she carried.

Helena's brow furrowed. "Why? What's your connection to this place?"

Violet's gaze met Helena's, revealing a cryptic knowing. "I've seen many attempted rebellions over the years. Serena used to use this armoury too, you know."

Helena's mind spun with questions, Serena's seemingly loyal facade now in question. "What do you mean? Serena was part of a rebellion?"

Violet only offered a mysterious smile, leaving Helena standing alone in the hidden chamber, grappling with the fragments of information that hinted at a deeper, more intricate history within the Nest. As Violet scurried away down the hallway, her words lingered in the air, leaving Helena to ponder the enigmatic secrets that surrounded her.

The clinking of metal echoed through the hidden armoury as Helena turned toward the entrance. Genevieve, a regal and imposing figure, entered with a grace that seemed to command the very air around her. Helena, fueled by newfound curiosity and a thirst for understanding, confronted Genevieve with a question that had been gnawing at the edges of her thoughts.

"Genevieve," Helena began tentatively, "what happened to Serena? Why is she the way she is now?"

Genevieve paused, her piercing gaze assessing Helena before she finally spoke. "Serena Springwell, once the greatest fighter this rebellion has ever known. We fought side by side against the vampires who held us captive." There was a fleeting sadness in Genevieve's eyes, a reflection of the shared history she had with the seemingly carefree Serena.

Helena leaned forward, a mix of apprehension and determination etched on her face. "What happened to her?"

A heavy silence hung in the air as Genevieve's cold gaze met Helena's. "Serena endured unimaginable pain, Helena. The vampires, they took everything from her. Tortured her, broke her spirit. It was a fate none of us would wish upon our worst enemies."

The weight of Genevieve's words settled on Helena's shoulders, a revelation that Serena's carefree demeanour masked a past fraught with suffering. "But why is she here now? Why is she—"

Genevieve cut her off with a chilling tone. "Do you really want to know what happened? The details are gruesome, Helena. It's a darkness that some can never escape."

Helena hesitated, her eyes reflecting a mix of fear and curiosity. Despite the ominous warning, she nodded slowly, signalling that she was prepared to delve into the painful truths that lurked beneath Serena's surface.

"Serena Springwell's tale is one of tragedy and survival," Genevieve began, her voice steady but tinged with sorrow. As she unravelled the narrative of Serena's past, Helena listened intently, the weight of Serena's history settling into her own consciousness, reshaping her understanding of the rebels around her.

In the dimly lit armoury, the air was thick with an ominous anticipation as Genevieve began weaving the tapestry of Serena Springwell's painful past, unravelling a tale that had left indelible scars on the seasoned rebel fighter.

The armoury's walls seemed to melt away, replaced by the haunting echoes of a bygone era. The torchlight flickered, casting eerie shadows on the resolute faces of Serena and Genevieve. Swords drawn, their eyes bore the weight of their rebellion, poised for a climactic confrontation with the vampiric tyrant that held them captive.

Yet, the tableau of defiance crumbled, twisted by an unforeseen twist of fate. From the shadows emerged vampires, dark minions of Edward, dragging Serena's two sons into the cruel spotlight. The children's innocent faces, painted with terror, mirrored Serena's own anguish.

A malevolent voice pierced the air, the harbinger of despair, Vladimir—the sinister executor of Edward's malevolent whims. "Drop your weapons, or watch your sons die," he declared with a chilling detachment.

The world seemed to compress into that agonising moment, where the cruel realities of vampire tyranny eclipsed the rebels' hopeful defiance. Serena, torn between loyalty to the rebellion and the unbearable weight of maternal love, made the gut-wrenching decision to lower her sword. Her eyes pleaded with Genevieve to follow suit, to spare the lives of her beloved sons.

"No, Serena," Genevieve's voice cut through the tension, a defiant refusal to surrender. "We can't give in. We can't let them win."

The air crackled with desperation as Serena, overwhelmed by a torrent of emotions, lunged at Genevieve in a desperate attempt to force her compliance. The impact sent them both crashing to the ground, the clang of swords replaced by the gut-wrenching realisation of a mother's sacrifice.

In the cruellest of twists, Vladimir seized the opportunity. Cold and unfeeling, he executed the vampiric decree. Serena's sons, the embodiment of innocence, fell victim to the vampires' brutal machinations. Their lives extinguished, their blood staining the ground, and Serena's heart shattered into a million irreparable pieces.

Back in the present, the armoury stood as a silent witness to the echoes of a tragedy that reverberated through time. Genevieve, her eyes reflecting the haunted corridors of her own guilt, confessed with a heavy heart. "I've never felt so sorry for someone as I did

Serena Springwell. We were in love, you know, Edward and I. But I betrayed him, and Serena paid the price. I should have stabbed him through the heart when we had the chance... or at least stabbed myself so I wouldn't have to continue with his torment." The air hung heavy with the weight of the past, and the armoury's walls seemed to absorb the pain and remorse etched into Genevieve's voice. Helena, a silent observer to Serena's anguish, felt the gravity of the rebellion's history—the cost of freedom measured in the blood of innocent lives lost in the ceaseless struggle against the vampiric oppressors.

The courtyard lay bathed in the soft glow of twilight, its serenity masking the undercurrent of secrets and tension that pervaded the Nest. Helena, her determination unyielding, sought answers in the fading light. She found Serena Springwell lingering near a marble fountain, seemingly lost in her own enigmatic world. "Serena," Helena called, her voice cutting through the tranquil air. As she approached, Serena turned to face her, her vacant smile failing to conceal the weight of hidden truths.

"What can I help you with, dear?" Serena's voice carried an unsettling sweetness, a practised veneer of innocence that Helena saw through.

Helena squared her shoulders, confronting the woman who, despite her current facade, had once been a formidable rebel warrior. "I know who you were, Serena. A great fighter, a leader among the rebels. What happened to you?"

Serena's smile faltered imperceptibly, but she quickly recovered. "I'm afraid you have me confused with someone else, my dear. I've always been devoted to our gracious hosts."

Frustration surged within Helena, her resolve unwavering. "Don't play games with me. I've heard the stories. You were a warrior, strong and fierce. What happened?"

Serena's eyes flickered, a hint of recognition breaking through the carefully constructed facade. Yet, she maintained her charade, denying her past. "I think you've been listening to too many fairy tales, my dear. I'm just a humble Blood Bride."

Growing impatient, Helena shook her head. "I expected more from you, Serena. Your rebel sons would be disappointed."

Serena's vacant expression shifted, her smile replaced by a sudden sternness. "Turn around. Get here. You have one chance."

Helena, surprised by the abrupt change, turned back to face Serena. The once-languid atmosphere morphed into one of expectancy. Serena's eyes, now ablaze with a hidden fire, held Helena in a piercing gaze.

"I will not fight," Serena declared, her voice low and resonant, "but if you wish to fight, I will show you how."

Helena felt a chill run down her spine as she glimpsed the shadow of the formidable rebel leader that Serena had once been. In that moment, a silent understanding passed between them, a shared acknowledgment of a history buried beneath layers of deceit. Serena agreed to secretly train Helena, a tacit attempt to reclaim a fragment of her old warrior spirit and pass it on to the one seeking answers. The courtyard, witness to the unspoken pact, held the promise of revelations yet to unfold.

Serena led Helena into the secluded gardens, bathed in the silver glow of the moon. A gentle breeze carried the scent of blooming flowers, masking the oppressive air of the Nest. There, beneath the celestial canvas, Serena and Helena embarked on their clandestine journey into the world of combat training.

The garden seemed to hold its breath as they approached a small clearing, surrounded by moonlit foliage. Serena's gaze lingered on the ancient trees that witnessed the unfolding stories of countless Blood Brides. With an air of solemnity, she reached down and picked up two stout sticks, offering one to Helena.

The sticks were simple, yet in Serena's hands, they became extensions of her formidable will. Helena eyed her opponent cautiously, uncertainty shadowing her features.

"I won't go back to that cursed room," Serena murmured, her eyes briefly flitting towards the direction of the armoury. "There are too many ghosts in there."

Helena nodded, understanding Serena's aversion. They moved to the centre of the clearing, the moonlight casting dynamic shadows as they assumed their positions. The initial clash of sticks echoed through the garden, an orchestral overture to their clandestine dance.

Serena moved with the grace of a seasoned warrior, her every motion deliberate and controlled. Helena, though less experienced, met Serena's strikes with determination, her movements fueled by a newfound determination. The sticks collided, the rhythmic symphony of their training reverberating through the night.

As they were spared, Helena's initial hesitation melted away. The sticks became extensions of their unspoken camaraderie, each clash forging an invisible bond. Serena's eyes, which had initially held a flicker of melancholy, now gleamed with a spark of vitality, a testament to the warrior she once was.

In the midst of the training, a peculiar laughter emerged—a shared cadence that transcended the oppressive atmosphere of the Nest. Serena, her laughter like a melody long unheard, shared a genuine smile with Helena. The laughter rippled through the moonlit clearing, a cathartic release of pent-up emotions.

"It's been ages since I've fought like this," Serena admitted, a mixture of nostalgia and newfound mirth in her eyes. "Feels good to be swinging sticks with a sister again."

Helena, still catching her breath, mirrored Serena's sentiment with a tentative smile. The moonlit garden bore witness to their unconventional bonding, a testament to the strength that emerged in the face of adversity. The sticks, once symbols of conflict, became instruments of connection, weaving an unspoken thread of understanding between Serena and Helena.

In the shared laughter and the rhythmic dance of combat, they discovered an unexpected refuge within the Nest's confinements—a fleeting moment of liberation beneath the silvered branches of the ancient trees.

Nikolai's voice cut through the night, interrupting the rhythmic dance of sticks in the moonlit garden. Helena and Serena froze, the echoes of their camaraderie lingering in the air as they turned to face him.

A flicker of suspicion danced in Nikolai's eyes as he observed the scene before him. His gaze flicked between Helena and Serena, the sticks in their hands, and the moonlit clearing that seemed to hold secrets.

"What are you doing out here?" Nikolai's voice, though calm, carried an undertone of curiosity.

Helena, quick to react, lowered her stick and approached Nikolai with a serene expression. "Just some calming yoga and meditation," she explained, her words carrying a soothing lilt.

Nikolai's brow furrowed, his suspicion lingering. "Yoga?" he questioned, eyeing the sticks in their hands.

"Yes, it's a form of meditation," Helena insisted, maintaining an air of innocence. "Serena was teaching me some techniques to find inner peace."

Serena, her stoic expression unwavering, nodded in agreement. "Yes, we thought the garden would be a serene setting for such practices."

Nikolai's gaze shifted between them, and after a lingering moment, he seemed appeased. "Very well," he conceded, a hint of uncertainty still lingering. "Helena, I'll be in the library when you're ready. We have matters to discuss."

Helena nodded, the tension in the air dissipating as Nikolai turned and walked back towards the Nest. As he disappeared into the shadows, Helena shot Serena a grateful glance.

"Thanks for covering for me," Serena muttered, her eyes reflecting a mix of gratitude and defiance.

Helena smirked, a newfound sense of camaraderie blooming between them. "We've got each other's backs," she replied, twirling the stick in her hand with newfound confidence. "Let's keep practising."

Serena nodded, and the moonlit garden once again became a sanctuary of shared laughter and the rhythmic dance of sticks—a secret haven amidst the shadows of the Nest.

The library, with its towering shelves and musty scent of ancient knowledge, welcomed Helena as she stepped into its embrace. Moonlight filtered through the ornate windows, casting a silvery glow over the countless volumes that lined the walls. Helena's fingers trailed over the spines of leather-bound books, each one a potential refuge from the haunting reality of the Nest.
Amidst the hushed whispers of parchment and the subtle creaking of shelves, Helena's ears caught a soft rustle. Turning towards the source, she discovered Violet, hidden amongst the shadows like a ghost. Her pale eyes flickered with a mix of surprise and vulnerability.
"Violet?" Helena called out softly, her voice echoing in the quiet space.
Violet started, her eyes widening before recognition set in.
"Helena," she replied hesitantly, stepping into the dim light.
Helena approached her with a warm smile, realising Violet had been seeking refuge in the sanctuary of books just as she had. "I

didn't expect to find anyone else here at this hour. Can't sleep either?"

Violet nodded, her gaze flickering nervously to the ornate door leading to the library. "I come here sometimes to escape," she confessed, her fingers tracing the cracked leather of an old tome. Helena's empathy deepened, understanding the need for a secret retreat within the oppressive confines of the Nest. "Me too," she admitted, "Books are like portals to another world."

The two shared a moment of silent camaraderie, their connection forged through the unspoken language of escapism. As Helena began to speak of her favourite stories, Violet's guarded demeanour softened. They delved into the tales that offered solace and strength, momentarily forgetting the grim reality that lurked outside the library's haven.

However, a sudden noise outside the door shattered the tranquillity. Violet's eyes widened in panic, and she darted behind a bookshelf as if fearing discovery.

"What's wrong?" Helena whispered, her concern mirrored in her eyes.

Violet, though visibly anxious, motioned for Helena to stay quiet. Helena strained her ears, and through the door, she heard the distant footsteps and low murmur of voices. The library, usually a sanctuary, now felt like a fragile haven on the brink of exposure. Violet's eyes met Helena's, a silent plea for secrecy. They remained hidden among the shelves, their breaths synchronised with the rhythm of the approaching footsteps. The library, once a sanctuary for shared stories, now sheltered a clandestine bond born from the shared fear of discovery in the oppressive heart of the Nest.

The library, once an oasis of quiet reflection, echoed with the soft shuffle of feet as Serena stepped inside. Her presence seemed to ripple through the room, the weight of memories hanging in the air like a subtle fragrance.

Serena approached Helena, a gleam in her eyes, a hidden promise. "I found something for you," she said, producing a sheathed dagger from within the folds of her cloak. It was a blade that bore the scars of a rebellious past, etched with stories of defiance and courage.

"This dagger belonged to me during the old rebellion," Serena explained, her voice a low murmur. "It's time for it to serve its purpose once again. Finish what we started."

Helena accepted the dagger with a mixture of reverence and determination. She could feel the weight of history in her hands, a silent pact forged by rebels long gone. The blade gleamed with untold stories, and as she unsheathed it, the metallic whisper cut through the quiet like a clarion call to action.

As Serena turned her gaze towards Violet, who had been hiding in the shadows, the corners of her lips curled into a warm smile. "Hi, Violet," she greeted, a genuine fondness in her voice. Violet hesitantly waved back, her eyes reflecting a blend of surprise and relief.

Just as Serena was about to ask another question, the library's heavy door slammed shut with a resounding echo. The sudden noise jolted the trio into an alert stance, their eyes narrowing with shared tension. The hallowed sanctuary of the library, where secrets and resistance converged, now held an unexpected intrusion, casting a veil of uncertainty over their clandestine meeting.

The room fell into a suspenseful silence, the air charged with the unspoken question of who had disrupted their clandestine gathering and what consequences might follow. In the ensuing stillness, the shadows seemed to deepen, cloaking the library in an ominous shroud, and the three rebels braced themselves for the unknown challenge that awaited just beyond the door.

The heavy door swung open with a creak, revealing an agitated Nikolai. His entrance marked an abrupt end to the clandestine meeting, the delicate equilibrium disrupted by his domineering presence.

Violet, sensing the sudden tension, hurriedly retreated from the library, leaving Nikolai to address the remaining rebels. He turned his stern gaze toward Serena, the air thickening with unspoken tension. Without a word, he commanded, "Leave."

Serena, resigned but unbroken, met Nikolai's gaze for a moment before turning on her heel and making her exit. The heavy door closed behind her, muffling the sound of her footsteps as she disappeared into the echoing corridors of the Nest.

Alone with Helena, Nikolai's attention shifted to the Swan who had dared defy his command. "Stop interacting with her," he ordered, his voice edged with anger. Helena, however, refused to bow to his wishes, her defiance simmering beneath her surface. In a sudden burst of rage, Nikolai seized Helena and barked, "Stay away from her!" His grip was forceful, and he threw her to the ground with a brutal disregard for her well-being. Pain seared through Helena's body as she struggled to her feet, her defiance burning brighter in the face of Nikolai's oppression.

Without another word, Helena fled from the library, the Lavender Suite offering the refuge she sought. The door closed behind her with a muted thud, leaving Nikolai alone in the quiet library. The lingering echoes of the confrontation hung in the air, a silent testament to the growing tension within the Nest, a tension that threatened to unravel the carefully woven threads of control that Nikolai sought to maintain.

Chapter Eight

A Child Was Born

The Lavender Suite enveloped Helena in a hushed ambiance, the air heavy with uncertainty as she lay on her bed, thoughts swirling like a tempest in her mind. The door creaked open, revealing the silhouette of Nikolai, the vampire who had just moments ago lashed out in a fit of anger. His presence hung in the room like a shadow, and Helena eyed him with a mixture of trepidation and wariness.

Nikolai approached, his expression softened by an unusual sincerity. "Helena," he began, his voice carrying an apologetic tone. "I must apologise for my harsh words. I care deeply for you, and my emotions got the better of me."

Helena remained silent, her distrust evident in her gaze. She braced herself for whatever explanation he might offer, a sense of unease settling within her.

Nikolai took a deep breath, as if preparing to unravel a long-held secret. "Violet," he revealed, "is my daughter. She was conceived with a human lover, Adelaide, from my past. I know it's a lot to take in, but I need you to understand."

Helena's eyes widened with surprise, the revelation catching her off guard. "Your daughter?" she repeated, her voice a mixture of disbelief and scepticism. "Why was she hiding in the library? Why keep her existence a secret?"

Nikolai sighed, sitting down on the edge of Helena's bed. "Violet is my weakness," he admitted, his eyes reflecting a complicated mixture of emotions. "I've hidden her away to protect her from the dangers of our world. I feared that others, including Edward, would exploit her if they knew."

Helena's distrust lingered, but curiosity gnawed at her. "Tell me everything," she demanded, her voice firm. "No more secrets."

Nikolai nodded, understanding the weight of the request. "Very well," he said. "Sit down; it's a long story, and you deserve to know the truth." As Helena settled into a chair, Nikolai began to unravel the intricacies of his past, revealing a narrative that intertwined love, loss, and the complexities of the vampire world.

The truth, it seemed, was a labyrinth Helena was just beginning to navigate.

Many Years Ago... the quaint, idyllic Happy Town unfolded before Nikolai's eyes, its facade concealing the orchestrated reality of a suburban utopia. It was in this staged paradise that he first laid eyes on Adelaide, a human woman who would forever alter the course of his existence. The atmosphere buzzed with the simplicity of happiness, the scent of blooming flowers filling the air.

Adelaide, a vision of warmth and genuine joy, approached Nikolai with a radiant smile that echoed through the picturesque streets. "Nikolai," she greeted, her voice carrying a melody of affection. "It's been too long."

Nikolai reciprocated her smile, his icy exterior momentarily thawed by the sincerity of her presence. "Adelaide," he murmured, the name rolling off his tongue like a cherished secret. "It feels like an eternity when I'm away from you."

The two lovers strolled through the Happy Town, hand in hand, their connection woven into the very fabric of the staged reality around them. Laughter echoed from the programmed townsfolk, painting a picture-perfect scene of suburban bliss.

As the sun dipped below the horizon, casting hues of orange and pink across the sky, Adelaide invited Nikolai into her home. The door closed behind them, shutting out the façade of happiness that enveloped the Happy Town.

In the intimate haven, Nikolai and Adelaide exchanged soft glances, the unspoken language of their affection bridging the gap between their worlds. "I missed you," Adelaide confessed, her fingers gently tracing the contours of Nikolai's face.

Nikolai pulled her into a tender embrace, their lips meeting in a passionate kiss that transcended the boundaries of their disparate existences. The room seemed to shimmer with the intensity of their connection as they succumbed to the warmth of shared desire.

As night fell, Nikolai and Adelaide lay entwined, the boundaries between vampire and human momentarily blurred in the cocoon of their love. "Stay with me," Adelaide whispered, her words echoing through the room.

Nikolai pressed a lingering kiss to her forehead. "I wish I could," he admitted, a twinge of regret underlying his words. "But duty calls, and I must return to the Nest."

Adelaide's gaze held a mixture of understanding and sorrow. "Promise me you'll come back," she implored, her eyes searching for a commitment that transcended the limitations of their worlds.

Nikolai nodded, a solemn promise etched into his expression. "I'll find a way," he vowed, his voice carrying the weight of his devotion.

As the flashback faded, the remnants of their love lingered in Nikolai's memory, a poignant reminder of a time when happiness felt unburdened by the complexities that awaited them.

The weeks flew by like fleeting moments of happiness, and as the shadows of reality encroached, Nikolai returned to the Happy Town. The once-lively streets seemed to lose their vibrant hues as he made his way to Adelaide's home, his heart weighted with both anticipation and trepidation.

Adelaide greeted him with a smile, though a subtle tension lingered in the air. The realisation that their union had consequences weighed heavily on both their hearts. As they entered her quaint kitchen, Nikolai's eyes met Adelaide's, silently acknowledging the gravity of the situation.

"I've been feeling different," Adelaide confessed, her hand subconsciously resting on her abdomen. "I think I might be pregnant."

Nikolai, a mixture of emotions flooding his immortal senses, suggested they perform a test together. With a bowl, sugar, and a vial of Adelaide's urine, they waited anxiously for the telltale signs. As the liquid mixed with the sugar, forming lumps in a silent confirmation, the room felt suspended in time.

Adelaide's eyes welled with tears, a cascade of conflicting emotions etched across her face. "It's true," she whispered, her voice trembling. "I'm carrying our child."

The revelation, while a testament to their love, cast a foreboding shadow over their happiness. Reluctantly, Nikolai informed Adelaide of the impending consequences. "I must tell the leaders of my kind about this," he explained, a heavy burden in his voice. "They won't allow a human-vampire hybrid to exist."

Adelaide's face paled as the gravity of their reality sank in. "What will happen to us?" she asked, fear and desperation lacing her words.

Nikolai's eyes, filled with a deep sadness, met hers. "They'll take you to the Nest," he confessed. "You won't be allowed to keep the child."

The news hung in the air like a dark cloud, casting a pall over their dreams of a shared future. The once vibrant Happy Town seemed to echo their sorrow, a reflection of the inevitability that awaited them. As they clung to each other in the fading light, the weight of impending separation settled over their hearts, the cruel consequence of love in a world divided by immortality and mortality.

Months passed like an eternity within the dark walls of the Nest, and the air itself seemed to carry the weight of sorrow. In a dimly lit chamber, surrounded by Blood Brides who cared for her, Adelaide went through the trials of childbirth. The room echoed with her pained cries, and each scream seemed to pierce Nikolai's very soul.

He was forced to watch from afar, a silent spectator to the agony of the woman he loved, the mother of his child. The dim light flickered like a fading hope, and Nikolai's heart ached with an indescribable pain. Violet, the symbol of their love, was about to enter the world under the shadow of captivity.

Adelaide's screams filled the air, and the Blood Brides, bound by their own fates, did what they could to help. The room felt like a battleground, a place where life and death collided in a cruel dance. In moments of respite, Adelaide's eyes, glazed with pain, sought out Nikolai's, silently pleading for comfort that he was unable to provide.

"I'm dying, Nikolai," she uttered between strained breaths, her words carrying the weight of an impending farewell. "I can feel it. I'm dying."

The room fell into an agonising silence as Adelaide's life ebbed away. Violet, the newborn embodiment of their love, cried her first breaths, but the joy was tainted by the grief that enveloped Nikolai. He was separated from the woman who had given him a reason to defy his immortal nature, and the agony of helplessness etched lines of torment on his immortal face.

As Adelaide's life force faded, leaving her with the last breaths of her existence, Nikolai was left with an indelible pain. The walls of the Nest seemed to close in, bearing witness to the tragedy that unfolded within its heartless confines. The echoes of Adelaide's final moments lingered, a haunting melody that would forever resonate within the depths of Nikolai's immortal soul.

The meeting room in the Nest, cold and imposing, hosted a tense negotiation between Nikolai and Edward. The air hung heavy with unspoken grievances and the weight of the decisions that would shape the future.

Nikolai's eyes bore the weariness of countless years and the depth of his love for the child he had lost. He pleaded with Edward, his voice carrying a mixture of desperation and determination.

"Please, Edward, I beg you. Let me raise her. She's innocent in all of this."

Edward, seated across the table, studied Nikolai with a stoic expression. The room seemed to hold its breath as the powerful vampire leader contemplated the request. After a prolonged silence, he finally spoke, his words dripping with reluctant acquiescence, "Very well, Nikolai. You may have her."

A glimmer of hope ignited in Nikolai's eyes, but it was quickly extinguished as Edward continued, revealing the true cost of this concession. "However, she will remain here, in the Nest, as leverage. A reminder of your allegiance."

Nikolai's shoulders slumped under the weight of the condition. He nodded, accepting the terms, though the ache in his undead heart deepened. As the negotiations concluded, Edward leaned forward, his piercing gaze locking with Nikolai's. "And one more thing," he added, "you will never tell her the truth. I will compel you to forget, and you will never reveal your true connection."

A heavy silence followed as Nikolai comprehended the full extent of the sacrifice he was making. He knew the consequences of defying Edward were dire, and the price he paid for his daughter's continued existence was his own silence. The weight of the vow settled upon him like an unbreakable chain, binding him to a lifetime of secrecy and longing.

Reluctantly, Nikolai nodded in agreement, sealing his fate as the silent guardian of a secret that would define his existence. The room, witness to countless schemes and secrets, absorbed the weight of this pact, and the echoes of a father's silent agony reverberated within its cold, stone walls.

The passage of years within the Nest brought both the routine of immortal existence and the fleeting moments of clandestine fatherhood for Nikolai. In the dimly lit chambers hidden away from prying eyes, he orchestrated makeshift childhood experiences for Violet. Each moment, a fragile treasure bound by the constraints of secrecy.

On one occasion, the walls echoed with laughter as they dipped brushes into vibrant paints, creating fantastical scenes on an old canvas. Nikolai marvelled at Violet's artistic expressions, her imagination painting worlds beyond the stone confines of their hidden sanctuary.

In another stolen moment, the clatter of wheels resonated through the hall as Violet clumsily manoeuvred a rusty old bicycle. Nikolai steadied her as she wobbled, the narrow corridor transformed into a fleeting memory of a bike ride under the moonlit sky.

The haunting melody of a piano echoed through the hidden chambers, the keys caressed by Violet's fingers under Nikolai's watchful eye. Music became a shared language, a connection beyond the unspoken truth that lingered in the shadows.

As the years unfurled, Nikolai found himself entangled in the delicate threads of paternal love. Yet, an inevitable sorrow lingered on the periphery, a silent reminder of the distance between them. The weight of the unspoken truth became an ever-present burden.

Then came the day when Violet, oblivious to the hidden complexities of her lineage, innocently called him "Brother." The words, though spoken with affection, carved through Nikolai's immortal heart. A bittersweet ache settled within him, a poignant reminder of the role he was forced to play.

The charade continued, a dance of stolen moments and suppressed emotions, as Nikolai navigated the intricate web of secrecy. In the shadows, he watched over Violet, his daughter by blood but bound by the shackles of a lie that threatened to unravel the fragile tapestry of their hidden world.

In the dimly lit Lavender Suite, the weight of centuries hung in the air, overshadowed by the secrets that bound the Blood Brides. As Nikolai poured out his heart, a plea woven with the threads of fatherly love and the limitations of a sire bond, Helena listened intently.

The narrative unfolded like an ancient tapestry, revealing the forbidden chapters of Nikolai's clandestine life with Violet. His voice resonated with the pain of a father who yearned to break the shackles of silence but found himself ensnared by the unyielding commands of his maker.

Helena, caught between the intricate complexities of their supernatural existence, contemplated the gravity of Nikolai's request. She saw in his eyes the desperation of a father whose heart ached to share the truth with his beloved daughter, to bridge the chasm that separated them.

After absorbing the tale of Violet's clandestine upbringing, Helena made her decision. She recognized the genuine love that Nikolai harboured for his daughter, and a sense of empathy welled up within her. Violet deserved to know the truth, to untangle the web of deception that had shrouded her existence.

Rising from her seat, determination etched across her features, Helena declared her intent. "I'll tell her, Nikolai. She deserves to be happy, to know the truth about who you are to her." The room seemed to hold its breath as she moved toward the door, ready to unravel the secrets that had been woven into the fabric of Violet's life.

As she stepped into the corridor, a cascade of emotions swirled within her. The weight of responsibility pressed upon her shoulders, but a flicker of hope illuminated the path ahead. Helena steeled herself for the revelation that awaited Violet, a truth that could reshape the fragile connections within the Nest.

The library, a sanctuary of knowledge and hidden truths, bore witness to the revelation that would reshape the fragile bonds within the Nest. Helena, guided by the weight of responsibility, stood at the threshold of disclosure, with Nikolai standing silently behind her.

As she turned to face Violet, the girl she had come to know and care for, Helena took a deep breath, preparing to unravel the secrets that had been veiled in shadows for far too long. Her voice, steady but filled with empathy, broke the quiet tension in the room.

"Violet, I need you to listen. Nikolai is not your brother; he's your father."

Violet's eyes widened in disbelief, and she took a step back, shaking her head in denial. "No, that can't be true. Nikolai is my brother. We've always been together."

Nikolai, his gaze heavy with sorrow, stepped forward, but Violet held up a hand, her expression a mix of confusion and defiance. "Stop, Nikolai. I don't know what she's trying to do, but you're my brother. That's the truth."

Helena tried to approach her, to offer comfort in the face of unsettling revelations, but Violet retreated further. Her voice, laced with a mix of anger and hurt, echoed through the library. "If you were my father, you wouldn't let me hide in the shadows. You'd have fought for me. You're no father of mine."

With those words, Violet turned on her heel and fled from the library, leaving behind a heavy silence. Nikolai, left standing in the corner, bore the weight of a truth that had fractured the semblance of family he had cultivated. As the door swung shut, the library seemed to echo with the remnants of shattered illusions, and the Nest held its breath, suspended between the truth and the consequences that would inevitably follow.

The library, once a haven of secrets, now bore witness to a truth that had been unveiled, leaving Nikolai standing in the wake of Violet's departure. As the door closed behind her, Helena turned to him, a mix of empathy and reassurance in her eyes.

"I know this is hard for you, Nikolai," she said softly, approaching him with a comforting embrace.

Nikolai, his gaze heavy with the weight of newfound responsibility, sighed deeply. "I never thought it would come to this. I should have told her the truth long ago."

Helena tightened her embrace, offering solace in the face of a fractured bond. "You can still be there for her, Nikolai. It's never too late to be a real father to Violet."

He nodded, determination flickering in his eyes. "You're right. I won't let this revelation destroy us. I'll be the father she needs, starting now."

With those words, Helena felt the weight of his commitment. Nikolai, once bound by secrecy, now vowed to rebuild the fractured trust with his daughter. The journey ahead was uncertain, but in that moment, Helena believed in the possibility of redemption and healing.

As Nikolai gathered his resolve, Helena offered one last assurance. "Give her time, Nikolai. Trust takes time to mend. But I believe things will be alright."

Nikolai managed a faint smile, grateful for Helena's support. Together, they stood in the library, a space that had witnessed both secrets and revelations, as they braced themselves for the challenges that lay ahead.

Chapter Nine

Always a warrior

The training room buzzed with tension as the Brides endured the brutality of their "endurance" training, a twisted ritual designed to break their spirits and make them submissive to their vampire overlords. The instructor, a merciless enforcer, singled out a visibly shaken young Bride, tormenting her mercilessly.

The girl, already battered and bruised, struggled to maintain her composure as the instructor delivered a particularly vicious blow. The room fell silent, except for the sickening sound of the impact. The other Brides watched in horror and helplessness, their fear palpable.

As the instructor raised his hand again, a cruel promise of more pain, Serena emerged from the crowd like a force of nature. Her usual cheerful demeanour replaced by a fierce resolve, she stepped forward to confront the sadistic instructor. "You will not touch her," Serena declared, her voice cutting through the room with unwavering defiance.

The instructor, momentarily taken aback by this unexpected resistance, sneered at Serena's audacity. "Step aside, Springwell. This is none of your concern," he spat, raising his hand once more.

Serena, undeterred, firmly blocked his path, staring him down with unyielding determination. The room seemed to hold its breath as Serena refused to back down, her eyes locked onto the instructor's. The cruel silence was shattered by the instructor's enraged demand for her to move aside, threatening dire consequences.

"I won't let you continue this brutality," Serena retorted, her voice steady and resolute. The instructor, infuriated by her defiance, stormed off, vowing to report her insubordination to Edward. With the immediate threat gone, Serena turned her attention to the battered young Bride. Gently, she offered solace and comfort, becoming a beacon of hope in the darkened room. Tears streamed down the girl's face as she thanked Serena for the unexpected act of bravery.

Helena and the other Brides, inspired by Serena's courage, crowded around her. Serena had defied the cruelty that bound them all, and in that moment, she became a symbol of resistance. The room, once filled with the oppressive weight of submission, now crackled with a renewed sense of defiance. Serena had shown them that even in the face of brutality, there was strength to be found in standing together.

The training hall buzzed with a palpable tension as Edward, the foreboding leader, made his entrance. His six fingers were tightly wrapped around a twisted walking stick, and the atmosphere shifted into one of eerie anticipation. The Brides stood at attention, their eyes fixated on the approaching figure that held sway over their lives.

As Edward limped his way toward Serena, the very embodiment of his oppressive rule, a hushed silence fell over the room. The other Brides glanced at each other, sharing a collective sense of unease as they awaited the impending confrontation.

Serena, standing resolute in the face of the malevolent vampire, squared her shoulders and met Edward's gaze with unwavering determination. Her refusal to submit to his authority echoed through the hall, a small but fierce act of rebellion against the cruelty that permeated their existence.

"You don't own me, Edward. You don't own any of us!" Serena's voice cut through the silence, a defiant proclamation that hung in the air like a challenge. Her eyes burned with the intensity of someone who had found strength within vulnerability, and the glimmer of a smile betrayed her underlying resolve.

Edward's reaction was swift and brutal, a stark reminder of the consequences for defiance. His walking stick swung with unrelenting force, connecting with Serena's head and sending her crashing to her knees. The impact reverberated through the room, chilling the hearts of the Brides who witnessed the brutal act.

Undeterred, Serena tried to rise again, her spirit unbroken despite the physical toll. The defiance in her eyes flickered like a flame that refused to be extinguished. A ripple of fear swept through the other Brides, now forced into submissive silence as Edward seized Serena by her hair, pulling her ruthlessly to her feet.

The malevolent vampire revealed the power he held over Serena, a sinister grin playing on his lips. "You will be executed at sunset for causing unrest," he declared, the words hanging in the air like a death sentence. A shiver ran down the spines of those who bore witness to this terrifying display of authority.

With a malevolent glint in his eyes, Edward tightened his grip on Serena's hair, ensuring she felt the weight of his dominance. "May you die at the hands of Vladimir the Executor, just like your children did," he hissed, the words a venomous reminder of the past that sent a cold chill through the training hall. The insidious threat lingered in the air, casting a long shadow over Serena's fate and deepening the ominous atmosphere that enveloped the Nest. In the aftermath of Edward's proclamation, the training hall was left in an eerie quiet. The Brides exchanged anxious glances, realising that Serena's bold defiance had come at a steep cost. The imminent threat of execution cast a long shadow over the room, and the insidious presence of Vladimir's impending arrival heightened the ominous atmosphere.

As Edward departed with Serena in tow, his malevolent aura lingered, but an observant eye might have noticed subtle signs of weakness. The twisted grin on his face faltered for a brief moment, a fleeting hint that the poison coursing through his veins was beginning to take its toll. The very foundation of the oppressive

Nest seemed to tremble, setting the stage for an impending storm that would reshape the lives of its inhabitants.

The anticipation in the Nest grew thick as the Brides and vampires were summoned to stand upon the grand staircase. A hushed silence fell over the assembly, broken only by the echoing footsteps of approaching doom. Vladimir's sleek black limousine glided to a regal stop, the engine's purr signalling the arrival of the infamous Executor.

The limousine's door swung open, and Vladimir emerged in his finest suit, a vision of darkness and elegance. His eyes, sharp as obsidian, scanned the assembly, relishing the atmosphere of unease. In his hand, he carried a black case, undoubtedly containing the instruments of his deadly craft. The air was charged with an ominous energy as Vladimir made his way up the staircase.

A sly smile played on his lips as he locked eyes with Nikolai, who stood behind Helena, protective but visibly tense. "Hello, brother," Vladimir greeted with theatrical flair, his voice a low rumble that echoed through the halls. "What a sexy Swan you have there," he added, his gaze lingering on Helena with an unsettling intensity. The onlookers shifted uncomfortably, feeling the weight of Vladimir's gaze.

The vampire Executioner tilted his head, as if appreciating the performance he was about to deliver. "Come to my chambers, brother," he commanded, the words dripping with arrogance. "Bring the girl."

The Brides and vampires exchanged uneasy glances, knowing that Vladimir's presence promised nothing but chaos and cruelty. The theatricality of the moment served as a stark reminder of the power he wielded and the impending threat that loomed over the Nest.

Nikolai hesitated for a moment, a conflicted expression crossing his face, before leading Helena to Vladimir's opulent chambers. The room was adorned with dark velvet curtains, luxurious furnishings, and a chilling air of extravagance. Vladimir stood by a lavish bar, pouring drinks with exaggerated charm as they entered. "Welcome, brother! And who is this exquisite creature you've brought to my lair?" Vladimir's voice oozed false charm as he raised his glass in a mocking toast.

Nikolai, clearly uncomfortable, managed a strained smile but refrained from joining the toast. An awkward tension settled in the room as Vladimir turned up the volume on the raucous music that filled the space. He sauntered toward Helena, a predatory gleam in his eyes.

"Shall we, my dear?" Vladimir seized Helena's arm, pulling her forcefully into a dance. The room seemed to shrink as they twirled around, the aggressive rhythm matching the aggressive grip of Vladimir's hands. Helena tried to resist, but Vladimir's strength was overpowering.

Nikolai remained seated, his eyes averted, the internal struggle evident on his face. The aggressive dance continued, and Vladimir's hands roamed over Helena's body inappropriately, violating the boundaries of decency. Helena shot pleading glances at Nikolai, silently begging for intervention, but he seemed paralyzed by the presence of his menacing brother.

As the song came to an end, Vladimir released Helena with a flourish. He remarked casually, "I must go sharpen my execution weapons. Duty calls, you know?" With a predatory smirk, he left the room, leaving behind a sense of violation.

Helena, now alone with Nikolai, felt exposed and humiliated. She turned to him, searching for an explanation, but he avoided eye contact, his face reflecting shame and regret. The lingering echoes of Vladimir's unwelcome touch left a chilling residue in the air, a stark reminder of the darkness that surrounded them.

Helena's eyes burned with a mixture of anger and hurt as she confronted Nikolai. "How could you let him touch me like that?" Her voice was cold, cutting through the silence that lingered in the opulent chamber.

Nikolai remained silent for a moment, his gaze fixed on the floor, unable to meet Helena's accusatory eyes. Her next words cut through the air like a razor. "Would you let him touch Violet like that?"

His silence was shattered by a sharp retort. "No, of course not! I would never allow him near Violet like that," Nikolai snapped, a sudden edge in his voice.

The room felt heavy with the weight of unspoken truths. Nikolai, burdened by his own fears, finally began to unravel the haunting story that had left scars on his soul. "Vladimir... he's always been a monster. Even before he became a vampire." Nikolai's voice wavered, revealing the deep-seated fear that Vladimir instilled in him.

He continued with a tremor in his voice, recounting a nightmarish memory. "When we were just young boys, he drowned our little brother Aleksander in a puddle. I... I watched it happen. It was the worst thing I've ever seen in my life."

Helena's anger softened into a sombre understanding. She could see the torment etched on Nikolai's face as he revealed the gruesome truth of Vladimir's cruelty. In that moment, he wasn't just a vampire, but a haunted soul burdened by the sins of his past.

Nikolai pleaded with Helena, his eyes pleading for understanding and compassion. "I'm terrified of him, Helena. Please, I beg you, reach out to Violet. Warn her to be careful, to protect herself. She must hide from Vladimir's cruelty. I cannot bear to see him harm her."

As the weight of their shared past settled between them, Helena nodded in agreement, vowing silently to protect not only herself but also Violet from the malevolent grasp of Vladimir, the executor of nightmares.

The dimly lit halls echoed with hurried footsteps as Helena navigated through the labyrinthine Nest in search of Violet. Her footsteps mingled with the distant sounds of despair and suffering, creating an unsettling symphony of the captive Blood Brides. In her relentless pursuit, she caught sight of Violet darting through the corridors, an elusive wisp.

Just as Helena rounded a corner, Genevieve materialised before her, a stern expression etched on her face. In a swift motion, Genevieve's hand closed around Helena's wrist, halting her chase. The urgency in Genevieve's eyes was undeniable.

"We must put on a façade, Helena," Genevieve declared in a hushed tone. "Serena is about to face her execution. We must stand in solidarity with her, even if it means showing a face."

Helena's eyes widened with a mix of shock and sorrow. The weight of Serena's impending fate pressed heavily on her heart. Genevieve's grip on her wrist tightened, a silent vow passing between them.

"Vladimir may be a powerful vampire, but we will avenge Serena. We will destroy them all, Helena," Genevieve asserted, her voice resonating with determination.

As they walked through the halls towards the gardens, Helena felt the gravity of the situation settle upon her shoulders. The echoes of their footsteps were like a march, a quiet rebellion in the face of impending tragedy. The two women, bound by their shared grief and the desire for freedom, moved with a shared purpose.

"It is time for her execution," Genevieve reiterated, the words heavy with the weight of inevitability. Helena steeled herself for what lay ahead, knowing that they must navigate a delicate dance between resistance and survival. The gardens awaited them, bearing witness to a sombre display of unity among the Blood Brides.

Vladimir descended the platform, a sinister silhouette among the sea of chained Brides. The rhythmic chant, echoing their defiance, surrounded him like an insurmountable force. Unfazed, he moved through the crowd with predatory grace, eyes scanning the faces of the assembled Brides.

Reaching Serena's lifeless body, he bent down and, with a ghastly nonchalance, seized her severed head. The chanting persisted, but now there was a palpable undercurrent of tension as Vladimir returned to the stage, Serena's head cradled in his hands.

The courtyard held its breath, a collective anticipation hanging in the air. Vladimir lifted Serena's severed head high, an ominous silhouette against the darkening sky. The defiant voices of the Brides faltered for a moment, the sheer brutality of the scene arresting their vocal rebellion.

Vladimir's voice cut through the lingering echoes of the chant. "You listen...good." His gaze swept across the crowd, a predatory smile curling on his lips. "I think I might just stay here for a while. I like what I see. You're...delicate."

A hushed silence enveloped the courtyard as the Brides, their spirits momentarily dampened, gazed upon the lifeless visage of Serena held aloft by their oppressor. Vladimir's presence, cruel and domineering, cast a shadow over the defeated assembly.

The threat of further discipline hung in the air, stifling the flame of rebellion. The Brides, once united in defiance, now stood subdued and vulnerable under the looming gaze of their malevolent captor. The delicate threads of resistance trembled in the aftermath of Serena's execution, and the Nest, for a moment, quivered beneath Vladimir's ominous reign.

In the dimly lit Lavender Suite, Helena, Genevieve, and Ravenna gathered, their faces marked by grief and the lingering shock of Serena's brutal execution. The room echoed with the weight of loss, and the flickering candles cast long shadows on the walls. Wordlessly, Genevieve produced a bottle of aged wine, its rich aroma filling the air as she poured it into delicate glasses. The three women lifted their glasses, a sombre yet determined unity binding them together. The clink of glass against glass resonated through the room, a melancholic acknowledgment of their fallen comrade.

"To Serena," Genevieve intoned, her voice carrying a mixture of sorrow and resolve. The others echoed the sentiment, their eyes reflecting the shared pain of losing a sister in arms.

As the wine flowed, a heavy silence settled over the room. Each sip carried the bitter taste of rebellion stifled, but beneath the surface, a simmering determination lingered. Genevieve, with a wry smile, proposed another toast, her gaze flickering with a steely resolve. "To kill those who can't be killed," she declared, a solemn vow wrapped in the clink of their glasses. The room became a sanctuary for their shared grief and the nascent seeds of rebellion.

In that moment, their collective strength swelled, pushing back against the oppressive forces that sought to crush them. Helena, Genevieve, and Ravenna sat together, united by a common purpose. The memory of Serena's sacrifice fueled the embers of resistance within them. As they contemplated the challenges ahead, a quiet determination settled over the Lavender Suite—a quiet storm waiting to unleash itself upon the Nest and the monsters who ruled within its walls.

Chapter Ten

A Message Received

The moon hung low in the velvety night sky, casting a gentle glow over the Nest as the occupants slept. In the quiet corridors, where shadows danced with the flickering candlelight, Genevieve moved with purpose. Helena, unable to sleep and restless with the weight of recent events, watched from her window as Genevieve clandestinely navigated the maze of hallways.

Dressed in a cloak that seemed to absorb the darkness, Genevieve slipped a sealed envelope from beneath her garments. She approached a lone Blood Bride, a silent messenger in the covert network that sought liberation from their oppressors. Helena's heart quickened as she observed the exchange, her senses attuned to the gravity of the moment.

The letter passed from one set of hands to another, like a secret dance in the night. Each Bride in the chain played a vital role, unknowingly contributing to the salvation of their kind. Genevieve's calculated steps and the unseen whispers of rebellion echoed through the silent halls.

The letter, meticulously coded to conceal its true intent, held the key to contacting an outside ally—an elusive hunter sympathetic to their cause. The burden of hope rested on that piece of parchment, weaving its way through the intricate web of resistance.

Helena, her breath caught in anticipation, strained to see the final link in the chain. The last Bride discreetly slipped the letter into the hands of an inconspicuous figure—a trusted messenger who would deliver their plea to the waiting hunter beyond the Nest's confines.

As Genevieve melted back into the shadows, her mission accomplished, Helena felt a flicker of optimism. The night held secrets, and with each clandestine exchange, the rebels wove threads of resistance, preparing for the storm that would shatter the Nest's oppressive silence.

The air inside Helena's chamber felt heavy with the weight of recent events, and a faint knock at the door stirred her from her contemplation. She turned to find Nikolai entering, his concern etched across his face. The sombre atmosphere clung to the room like a shroud.

"Are you okay?" Nikolai inquired, his voice a soft murmur in the dimly lit space.

Helena, her eyes reflecting the turmoil within, shook her head faintly. The recent execution of Serena had left scars on their collective spirit, and the oppressive presence of Vladimir lingered like a malevolent spectre.

Nikolai stepped closer, attempting to reassure her. "Things will settle down. Vladimir will move on, and we'll be safe if we keep our heads down."

Helena, however, couldn't find solace in his words. She implored him to join the rebellion, to stand alongside those who sought to break free from the chains that bound them. "You won't be safe if you're not with us," she pleaded.

But Nikolai, his resolve unwavering, refused. "It's too dangerous. I can't risk it."

He turned to leave, leaving Helena with a growing sense of frustration and helplessness. Unable to accept his decision, she followed him out into the dimly lit corridor. Nikolai looked back at her, questioning her presence.

"If you won't join us, you can't know," Helena declared, her voice tinged with determination. The rebellion had become a beacon of hope for her, and she couldn't stand idly by while others fought for their freedom. With that, she left Nikolai standing in the corridor, the weight of uncertainty lingering in the air.

The dimly lit corridors of the Nest echoed with the soft padding of footsteps as Helena and Genevieve stealthily made their way towards the hidden entrance to the armoury. Ravenna, ever vigilant, stood guard, her sharp eyes scanning the surroundings for any signs of unwanted company.

As they reached the entrance, Helena cast a glance at Ravenna, who nodded in silent assurance. The heavy door creaked open, revealing the hidden arsenal within. The metallic scent of weapons hung in the air as the two women stepped into the dimly lit room.

"Alright, let's take inventory," Genevieve whispered, her eyes scanning the racks of weapons that lined the walls.

As they started cataloguing the weapons, Helena couldn't help but feel a mix of anticipation and apprehension. The weight of the rebellion rested on their shoulders, and the weapons they catalogued would soon be wielded by those who sought freedom. Curiosity gnawed at Helena, and she couldn't resist asking Genevieve, "What do you plan on doing with all these weapons?" Genevieve paused, glancing at Helena with a determined expression. "You saw those women chanting, right? Give an angry woman a weapon, and she will not back down. I trust my sisters. They may not have the training, but they are angry. Anger is a strong thing, Helena."

The words hung in the air, carrying the weight of the impending uprising. Helena nodded, understanding the power that could be unleashed when oppressed souls found a means to channel their anger. The armoury held not only weapons but the potential for rebellion and, hopefully, liberation.

The Lavender Suite, usually a sanctuary for the Brides, now became a clandestine armoury, filled with the hushed clinking of weapons and the muted whispers of rebellion. Helena, Genevieve, and Ravenna carefully carried armfuls of weapons, each step echoing the weight of their shared determination.

In the midst of this clandestine operation, a sudden commotion outside the suite drew their attention. The unmistakable sounds of violence echoed through the corridor, freezing them in their tracks. They exchanged uneasy glances, their expressions revealing a mix of fear and anger.

As the Lavender Suite's door creaked open, they saw Vladimir, the embodiment of cruelty, ruthlessly assaulting a young Bride. The atmosphere in the room shifted, the air heavy with tension and suppressed rage. Ravenna's instincts flared, and she moved towards the door, ready to confront Vladimir.

Genevieve, however, extended her arm, blocking Ravenna's path. "Not yet," she whispered, her eyes fixed on the scene unfolding outside.

The assault continued, leaving the young Bride battered and broken. Vladimir, savouring his brutality, finally departed, leaving the corridor stained with fear and agony. The moment he disappeared from view, Genevieve nodded to Ravenna, signalling that the time for action had not yet come.

Helena approached the injured Bride, her heart heavy with empathy. She gently brushed the girl's dishevelled hair, offering a silent vow for justice. The Lavender Suite, now housing an arsenal of defiance, became a haven of shared determination against the tyranny they faced.

Ravenna and Genevieve resumed their task, carrying the weapons into the suite, their eyes burning with a quiet fire. The assault they had witnessed only fueled the flames of rebellion within them. Vladimir's reign of terror would not go unanswered. The Lavender Suite, once a symbol of submission, now harboured the seeds of defiance, waiting to bloom into an uprising against the darkness that loomed over the Nest.

The Lavender Suite, usually a haven of shared secrets, now buzzed with whispered conversations as Helena entered. Genevieve and Ravenna were busy concealing the cache of weapons they had amassed, careful not to make a sound that might betray their covert activities.

As Helena approached, Ravenna's keen eyes caught sight of a familiar dagger among the weapons. The air seemed to still for a moment as she recognized it. "This... This is Serena's," she uttered, her voice laced with reverence and sorrow. Helena nodded, her eyes glistening with the weight of the memories tied to that blade. Genevieve, sensing the need for a shift in focus, gestured towards the assortment of weapons. "Serena left her mark on this rebellion, and now it's time we honour her memory. These weapons will be our voice," she declared, her gaze unwavering. Helena, eager to contribute, questioned, "But how will we distribute these? How can the Brides keep them hidden?" Ravenna, always resourceful and intuitive, took charge. "We'll need to teach them covert transport. Small weapons can be concealed within the folds of their dresses, and nobody would be the wiser."

Helena watched intently as Ravenna demonstrated, taking Serena's dagger and revealing a length of ribbon. With a few deft movements, she secured the dagger to her leg, the ribbon blending seamlessly with the fabric of her dress. It was a subtle yet effective method, ensuring that the Brides could carry concealed weapons without arousing suspicion.

"See, Helena?" Ravenna said, her eyes locking onto hers. "We adapt. We survive. And soon, we'll strike back."

Genevieve nodded in agreement. "The Brides will learn to carry more than just the burden of submission. These weapons will be a symbol of their strength and our collective will."

Helena, holding Serena's dagger in her hands, felt the weight of responsibility and determination settling on her shoulders. The Lavender Suite, once a place of secrets, had become a forge for the rebellion's arsenal. As they continued their preparations, the air in the room crackled with the anticipation of a storm about to break. The Brides were ready to reclaim their destinies, one hidden weapon at a time.

As the atmosphere in the Lavender Suite buzzed with tension, a thin envelope slid soundlessly beneath the door. Genevieve, quick to spot the unexpected delivery, picked it up with practised efficiency. The letter was adorned with cryptic symbols and coded language, a familiar sight that held the promise of hope.

Helena, intrigued by the mysterious correspondence, observed as Genevieve's eyes scanned the contents. "What's that?" she inquired, her curiosity piqued.

Genevieve, a mask of determination on her face, briefly met Helena's gaze before replying, "It's from our contact on the outside. He's confirmed. Tomorrow night, he'll be here."

A spark of optimism flickered in Genevieve's eyes, a rare sight in the midst of the gloom that surrounded them. Helena, though still uncertain about the mysterious figure, couldn't deny the contagious hope that radiated from Genevieve's conviction.

"Who is he?" Helena prodded, a mix of curiosity and caution in her voice.

Genevieve shook her head. "I don't know. He's kept himself hidden in the shadows, and for now, that's how it has to be. But he's our chance at freedom."

Eager to divert her thoughts, Helena suggested, "I'll go look for Violet. Maybe she needs to hear about this."

Genevieve nodded in agreement, issuing a quiet warning, "But be discreet. We can't afford any slip-ups."

As Helena exited the Lavender Suite, the dimly lit halls of the Nest stretched before her like a maze of secrets. She moved cautiously, her steps silent as she navigated the shadows. Violet's whereabouts remained unknown, but Helena's determination drove her forward, hoping to find her and share the glimmer of hope that had arrived in the form of a coded letter.

Helena, in her quest to find Violet, unwittingly stumbled upon a scene that sent shivers down her spine. The door to Edward's office stood slightly ajar, allowing her an unintended glimpse into the heart of darkness that lurked within the Nest.

Hesitant but unable to resist the morbid curiosity, Helena peeked inside. The room was dimly lit, casting eerie shadows on the faces of the two vampires within—Edward and Vladimir. They sat together, sharing an unholy camaraderie that sent a chill through Helena's veins.

As her eyes adjusted to the dim light, Helena's horror intensified. The room echoed with the twisted laughter of the malevolent duo, and the air was thick with the stench of their malevolence. On the desk before them lay a layout of the Nest, with names of Brides marked, presumably for their twisted amusement.

The vile conversation they exchanged about methods of punishment and torment was nauseating. Their laughter reverberated off the walls as they joked about inflicting pain on the Brides, proposing grotesque and sadistic ideas that made Helena's stomach churn.

"Perhaps we should devise a game," Edward suggested, his voice dripping with malice. "A game of pain and suffering, with each Bride serving as a pawn in our little theatre of cruelty."

Vladimir, his sadistic glee matching Edward's, chimed in, "Oh, I have a charming idea involving fire. The Brides will dance to the rhythm of their own agony."

The room resonated with their macabre suggestions, each proposal more grotesque than the last. Helena, overcome with terror and disgust, stumbled back from the doorway, her heart pounding in her chest.

As she retreated into the shadows of the corridor, she vowed to herself that she would do whatever it took to protect the Brides from the impending horrors that Edward and Vladimir plotted in their sadistic symphony of cruelty.

The dimly lit corridors of the Nest seemed to stretch endlessly as Helena searched for Violet, her heart pounding with worry. The echoes of Vladimir and Edward's twisted conversation still haunted her, and the urgency to find Violet grew with each passing moment.

As she explored the labyrinthine hallways, Helena's eyes caught sight of a hidden compartment in the wall. Pulling aside the concealing curtain of shadows, she discovered a small stuffed teddy bear tucked away. Panic seized her. Where was Violet? Helena frantically looked around, hoping to catch a glimpse of her friend.

Suddenly, a voice cut through the silence. "What are you doing here?" Helena's gaze shot upward to find Vladimir standing before her. His grin, a malevolent curve, sent shivers down her spine. "You shouldn't be walking around at these hours," Vladimir remarked with a mockingly concerned tone. "A Swan like you could lose her feathers flailing around in the dark."

Before Helena could react, Vladimir apprehended her, his grip firm and unyielding. He led her through the labyrinthine halls, their shadows stretching grotesquely along the cold, stone walls. As the dungeons loomed before them, Helena's mind raced. She couldn't afford to reveal her true intentions or the rebellion's plans.

In the damp and dimly lit dungeon cell, Vladimir began his brutal interrogation. His questions were laced with suspicion and malice, designed to break Helena's resolve. Yet, Helena remained steadfast. She avoided divulging any critical information, skillfully dodging his inquiries with cryptic answers.

The hours dragged on, the air in the dungeon heavy with tension. Despite the physical and psychological torment, Helena refused to let Vladimir's sadistic methods crush her spirit. She stared defiantly into the eyes of her tormentor, a silent vow to protect the rebellion burning in her eyes.

As the night wore on, Vladimir grew frustrated. Helena's resilience and refusal to yield left him with no choice. With a begrudging expression, he ordered the guards to release her. Helena emerged from the dungeon, battered but unbroken. Vladimir's suspicions lingered, but Helena's calculated responses had left him with no tangible evidence. She walked away, her resolve unshaken, knowing that the upcoming coup was more crucial than ever. Time was running out, and she needed to warn the rebellion about the impending threat Vladimir posed to their plans.

Chapter Eleven

The Father of Rebellion

Helena's limbs felt heavy and her steps were weary as she retraced the dimly lit corridors back to her chambers. The ordeal of 24 hours in Vladimir's interrogation had left her physically and mentally drained. As she approached her lavender suite, she noticed Ravenna waiting outside, a concerned expression etched on her face.

Ravenna acknowledged Helena's presence with a solemn nod. "He's meeting with Genevieve now," she said, her voice low and cautious.

A spark of hope flickered in Helena's tired eyes. The mention of the mysterious hunter brought a renewed sense of purpose. She needed to know more, to understand how they could escape this nightmarish existence.

"Can I go in?" Helena asked, her voice a mere whisper.

Ravenna knocked gently on the door, and after a moment, it creaked open. Genevieve stood on the other side, her eyes reflecting a mix of determination and urgency.

"You should come in now," Genevieve said, holding the door open for Helena. As Helena stepped into the room, the weight of uncertainty hung in the air. The hunter's revelations were poised to unfold, and with them, a glimmer of hope for the rebellion.

The room seemed to blur for a moment as Helena stepped inside. She was prepared to meet the hunter who held the promise of liberation, but the sight that greeted her left her stunned. The figure standing before her, rugged and worn from the passage of time, held a familiarity that transcended the years.

As their eyes met, a slow recognition dawned upon Helena. The lines etched on his face, the wild growth of his hair, and the weariness in his eyes all told a story of a man who had endured much since they last saw each other. And then, in a heartbeat, it struck her—this hunter, this mysterious saviour, was her father.

"Jim?" she whispered, her voice catching in her throat. Her eyes welled up with tears, unable to comprehend the miracle standing before her.

Jim Swanson, her father, moved forward, closing the distance between them. There was a palpable tension in the room, a blend of disbelief, joy, and a profound relief that after all the suffering, they had found each other once again.

Helena's legs carried her forward almost instinctively. As they met in a tearful embrace, the weight of the world seemed to momentarily lift. Their tears were not only of sadness but of the overwhelming joy of a reunion after enduring the unbearable.

After a moment, Jim pulled back, his hands cupping Helena's face as he looked into her eyes. "My sweet girl," he whispered, voice choked with emotion. "I never stopped looking for you. I love you, Helena."

Helena could hardly form words through the lump in her throat. "Dad," she managed, the single word holding a universe of emotions.

In that room, amid the shadows of rebellion and the echoes of Serena's sacrifice, father and daughter found solace in the embrace of their unexpected reunion.

Jim led Helena to a quieter corner of the room, away from prying eyes and the weight of their shared history. Genevieve, sensing the need for privacy, excused herself with a subtle nod.

"Helena," Jim began, his voice a mixture of paternal concern and the weight of untold stories, "I've been searching for you ever since that night. The night our lives were torn apart."

Helena nodded, tears glistening in her eyes. She'd been haunted by the memories of that fateful night, the terror of losing her family, the relentless pursuit by vampires, and the disappearance of Lucy Sparks. But now, in her father's presence, the pain seemed to find a release, a shared burden they could carry together.

Jim gently cupped Helena's face in his hands, his gaze searching hers. "I need to know, sweetheart. Are you okay?"

A small, sad smile graced Helena's lips. "It's been hard, Dad. But I'm okay. I've survived, just like you taught me."

He nodded, reassured yet pained by the acknowledgment of the hardships she endured. "And you? How did you survive? What happened after that night?"

Jim took a deep breath, reliving the anguish of the past. "After the attack, I fought back. I've been on the run, trying to stay one step ahead of them. But all that time, my only goal was to find you, to bring you back to safety."

Helena listened, her heart heavy with the weight of her father's sacrifices for her. Then, as a sudden thought gripped her, she asked the question that had lingered in her heart for years. "Lucy. Is she alive? Have you seen her?"

Jim's expression shifted, revealing the shadow of uncertainty. "I haven't seen her since that night," he admitted, his eyes reflecting the pain of an unanswered question.

Helena's tears fell freely now, a mixture of relief and sorrow. She clung to her father, finding solace in his embrace, even as uncertainty about Lucy's fate loomed overhead. In that moment, the reunion brought both comfort and the remainder of the unresolved pieces of their shared past.

Outside the closed door, Ravenna's eyes burned with a bitter intensity. The corridor felt oppressive, and she couldn't shake the resentment that gnawed at her insides. Helena, reunited with her father, was granted a moment of solace, a brief respite from the horrors of the Nest.

"She gets to escape, to be with her family," Ravenna seethed, clenching her fists, her frustration boiling over. "What about the rest of us, Genevieve? When do we get our chance to be free?"

Genevieve, always the calm presence, placed a hand on Ravenna's shoulder, attempting to temper the flames of her anger. "Ravenna, we're all in this together. Helena's reunion is a flicker of hope, a sign that our time is coming. We need to be patient and united."

But Ravenna, consumed by impatience and a burning desire for freedom, struggled to heed Genevieve's calming words. "I'm tired of waiting. Tired of watching others escape while we're stuck in this hell."

Genevieve's gaze held a mixture of understanding and concern. "Ravenna, the rebellion is gaining strength. We're preparing for the moment we can all break free. But we need to be strategic. Acting impulsively only puts us at risk."

A feral glint flickered in Ravenna's eyes. "Risk? We're already risking our lives every day. How much longer are we supposed to endure this torment?"

Genevieve sighed, recognizing the growing storm within Ravenna. "We're close, Ravenna. I can feel it. But we need everyone focused and disciplined. We can't afford to lose anyone."

As the door to Helena's room remained closed, the tension in the hallway mirrored the rising turbulence within Ravenna. The impending rebellion cast a shadow, and how they navigated these crucial moments would determine their fate. The Nest trembled on the brink of change, and Ravenna's struggle echoed the collective yearning for freedom that resonated among the Brides.

As Helena and Jim made their way down the corridor, the air seemed heavy with unspoken emotions. The Lavender Suite, once a haven and a battleground, was now a place of bittersweet farewells. Genevieve, a stalwart figure in the rebellion and a surrogate mother to Helena, stood by the door, her eyes glistening with unshed tears.

"My bird of prey," she whispered, her voice a delicate mixture of pride and sorrow. "Fly far and free, Helena. We'll be waiting for the day when all of us can soar together."

Helena turned to face Genevieve, her own eyes shimmering with gratitude and the weight of the impending separation. In that moment, the Lavender Suite felt like a sanctuary of shared pain and resilient hope.

"Thank you, Genevieve," Helena said, her voice steadied by the deep connection they had forged. "For everything. I won't forget." Genevieve approached, her arms enveloping Helena in a tender embrace. "You're like a daughter to me. Find your freedom, and when the time is right, we'll meet again. I believe in you, Helena." With a gentle squeeze, they parted. Ravenna, silent but watchful, nodded in acknowledgment. The corridor bore witness to the quiet strength that had bound these women together in their fight against oppression.

As Helena and Jim continued down the corridor, each step took them closer to the unknown, and the echoes of heartfelt goodbyes lingered in the air. The Lavender Suite stood silent, a witness to the resilience of those left behind and the hope that fluttered in the hearts of those venturing into the shadows.

The darkened halls of the Nest became a labyrinth as Helena and Jim navigated the shadows in search of Violet. Tension gripped the air, their clandestine escape plan slowly unravelling. As they turned a corner, a sinister figure emerged from the darkness — Vladimir, the formidable vampire enforcer.

"Going somewhere, Swans?" he sneered, his voice dripping with malice. Before they could react, Vladimir lunged at them, a blur of predatory grace. Jim, seasoned but worn, pulled out a stake, determination etched on his face, while Helena, desperate to protect her father, brandished a weapon she had picked up in the Lavender Suite.

The skirmish that followed was a chaotic ballet of clashes, grunts, and desperate manoeuvres. Jim fought valiantly, aiming the stake at Vladimir's heart, but the vampire's centuries-old instincts thwarted every move. Helena, despite her resolve, was overpowered by Vladimir's supernatural strength.

"You thought you could escape me?" Vladimir taunted, his laughter echoing in the narrow corridor. "You're just birds with clipped wings, destined to flutter in the cage I've built for you."

In the midst of the struggle, Vladimir landed a brutal blow to Jim's side, sending him sprawling to the cold floor. Helena, witnessing her father's pain, fought harder, fueled by a surge of adrenaline. But Vladimir, revelling in the dance of violence, effortlessly disarmed her.

"Your little rebellion ends here," Vladimir declared, seizing both Helena and Jim with an iron grip. He dragged them, battered and defeated, towards Edward's ominous chamber, where their failed escape would be exposed, and the consequences would be dire. The Nest, once again, proved an inescapable prison, its walls echoing with the sounds of shattered hope and the harsh reality of vampire tyranny.

The metallic tang of blood hung thick in the air as Edward, with an air of ruthless authority, ordered Vladimir to carry out the grim execution. Helena's father, Jim, knelt with grim resignation, his eyes locking with Helena's for a final, desperate connection.
"No!" Helena's scream echoed through the chamber as Vladimir, the cold executioner, raised his hand high, wielding a lethal blade with deadly precision. The blade came down, severing Jim's head from his shoulders, leaving Helena's world shattered.
A guttural cry of anguish tore from Helena's throat, her body convulsing with the horror of witnessing her father's demise. The pain was not just physical; it was a soul-rending torment that threatened to consume her.
Fuelled by an overwhelming surge of anger, Helena's instincts propelled her forward, propelled by a desperate desire to avenge her father. But Vladimir, his predatory reflexes unmatched, easily

thwarted her attack. With a swift and brutal counter, he incapacitated her, delivering a devastating blow that left Helena crumpled on the cold, unforgiving floor.

As darkness encroached upon her vision, Helena's consciousness slipped away. The last image imprinted on her mind was the lifeless form of her father, an innocent victim sacrificed in the name of vampire cruelty. The Nest, steeped in darkness and despair, held Helena captive in both body and spirit, her dreams of freedom shattered by the brutality of her captors.

Chapter Twelve

Locked In A Cage

Helena's eyes fluttered open, her body pulsating with pain.
The cold, damp air of the cellar enveloped her, and the realisation of her surroundings sank in. She was confined within a cage, an unwilling prisoner in the bowels of the Nest. Bruises adorned her body like morbid art, and a metallic taste lingered on her tongue. In the dim shadows, a figure emerged—Violet. Her silhouette cast an eerie presence, and as she timidly stepped forward, Helena's frustration boiled over. The pain, both physical and emotional, sought an outlet in her harsh words.
"What were you thinking?" Helena's voice crackled with anger as she glared at Violet. "I told you to stay hidden. You led us into a trap, and now my father is dead!"
Violet recoiled as if struck, her features obscured by the dim light. Hurt flickered in her eyes as she stammered, "I... I'm sorry, Helena. I didn't mean for this to happen."

The weight of guilt pressed down on Helena, but her pain and fury drowned any sympathy she might have felt. "Just go away, Violet. I don't want to see you."

Without uttering another word, Violet retreated into the shadows, leaving Helena alone in her cage, surrounded by the suffocating darkness that mirrored the desolation within her heart. The harsh reality of her captivity had never been more palpable, and the betrayal she felt seeped into every bruise and cut that adorned her battered body.

The heavy footsteps of Edward echoed through the stone cellar as he descended into the depths of the Nest. Vladimir followed closely, a sinister smile etched on his face. The cold, dimly lit space seemed to shrink further as they approached Helena's cage. Helena, still bruised and weakened, looked up as the cellar door creaked open. Dread settled in her chest, and the air grew thick with tension. Vladimir's eyes glinted with malevolence as he took in the sight of the captive Swan.

Edward's voice, dripping with authority, resonated through the cellar. "Vladimir, you have my permission to deal with her as you see fit. She needs to learn her place."

Vladimir's smile widened, revealing a sadistic satisfaction. He approached the cage with deliberate steps, relishing the anticipation of torment. Helena, though battered and weary, locked eyes with him defiantly.

"Remember, Helena," Edward sneered, "there are consequences for disobedience."

Vladimir raised an eyebrow, his gaze fixated on Helena. "Let's make this memorable, shall we?" he said, relishing the power granted by Edward.

As the cellar door closed behind them, Helena braced herself for whatever sadistic whims Vladimir had in store, knowing that the consequences of her defiance would be etched into her memory with every lash, both physical and psychological.

The cold, damp cellar became a chamber of torment as Vladimir, fueled by sadistic pleasure, unleashed his brutality upon Helena. Chains rattled as he tormented her, his hands leaving a trail of violence and violation. The air was thick with Helena's laboured breaths and the malevolent satisfaction emanating from Vladimir. As Helena teetered on the brink of losing consciousness, her battered body surrendering to the relentless assault, a dim light flickered in her blurry vision. Nikolai descended the stairs, his expression momentarily frozen in shock and horror at the scene unfolding before him.

"Nikolai!" Helena's voice, weakened and strained, croaked out the plea. The cruel dance Vladimir had orchestrated halted for a moment as the attention shifted.

Nikolai's eyes, a mix of revulsion and internal conflict, met Helena's gaze. There was a brief pause, a silent exchange laden with the weight of their shared history. The room hung in tense anticipation as Nikolai grappled with the conflicting emotions within him.

Vladimir, sensing an interruption, turned to face Nikolai with a wicked grin. "Ah, the obedient little brother. Joining the party, are we?"

Nikolai's fists clenched, a mix of anger and shame etched across his face. In that fleeting moment, Helena saw the struggle within him, torn between loyalty to his vampiric kin and the lingering humanity that still clung to his existence.

The cellar's oppressive silence shattered as Nikolai, unable to stand idly by, took a step forward, his jaw set in a silent promise. The confrontation that loomed in that dark, desolate space would determine the fates of those caught in the web of vampire politics and rebellion.

The cellar descended into a chaos of brutality and madness as Nikolai, fueled by a frenzied rage, unleashed a merciless assault upon Vladimir. Helena, confined within the cage, witnessed the gruesome ballet of violence, her eyes wide with a mix of horror and disbelief.

Vladimir, once the embodiment of sadistic power, now found himself at the mercy of Nikolai's unrestrained fury. The air crackled with the sounds of bones breaking, the wet thuds of impact, and Vladimir's desperate cries for mercy. Despite his pleas, there was no respite from the relentless onslaught.

Nikolai's eyes burned with a wild intensity, the crimson hue reflecting the tumultuous emotions that churned within him. Every strike, every blow, echoed the tumultuous history between the two brothers. In that moment of frenzied chaos, the boundaries of loyalty and family were shattered.

Driven by a mad love for Helena, Nikolai's assault escalated. The cellar became a theatre of violent retribution, a culmination of years of anguish and suppressed hatred. The lines between predator and prey blurred, and the once mighty Vladimir found himself reduced to a broken, bloodied shell.

With a final, gruesome twist, Nikolai, consumed by the intoxicating maelstrom of emotions, tore Vladimir's head from his shoulders. The grotesque spectacle unfolded before Helena's horrified eyes, a visceral and savage conclusion to a nightmarish chapter.

As the lifeless body of Vladimir crumpled to the ground, Nikolai, panting and covered in blood, turned his gaze toward Helena. In that tumultuous gaze, she saw a mixture of regret, relief, and a haunting acknowledgment of the irreversible path they had tread. The cellar fell into an eerie silence, punctuated only by the laboured breaths of the survivors and the lingering scent of violence that hung in the air. The twisted chapter had come to a close, leaving behind a macabre tableau of vengeance and the indelible stains of a love gone mad.

Chapter Thirteen

Talking About A Revolution

As Nikolai pulled Helena from the bloody cellar, his eyes still ablaze with the remnants of a murderous rage, she pleaded for her life. The wild, frenzied energy surrounding him sent shivers down her spine, and she feared becoming the next victim of his unchecked bloodlust.

"Hold on, please," she implored, her voice trembling. "You have to control yourself, Nikolai."

Gradually, as if awakening from a trance, Nikolai's gaze softened. His grip on Helena loosened, and he took a step back, regaining some semblance of control over the monstrous urge that had possessed him. A haunted look lingered in his eyes, the aftermath of the violence he had unleashed upon Vladimir.

They emerged into the chaos of the Nest manor, where the rebellion had erupted into a full-blown battle. Vampires clashed with Brides, the once pristine halls now transformed into a battleground. Furniture lay overturned, the air filled with the acrid scent of conflict and the symphony of screams and clashes. Helena's eyes widened at the pandemonium unfolding around her. The rebellion, fueled by the fiery spirit of defiance, had taken root within the very heart of the Nest. Genevieve's plan was in motion, and the cost of freedom was etched in the blood-soaked tapestry of the Nest manor.

"We have to find Genevieve," Helena shouted above the tumult, her voice barely audible over the chaos. Nikolai, still grappling with the aftermath of his violent outburst, nodded in agreement. Together, they navigated through the tumultuous scenes of battle, dodging confrontations between vampires and Brides.

As they ventured deeper into the heart of the rebellion, Helena couldn't shake the fear that the freedom they sought might come at an unimaginable cost. The Nest, once a fortress of oppression, was now a battlefield where the struggle for liberation unfolded with every clash and scream that echoed through its halls.

Helena and Nikolai pressed through the tumult, following the chaotic symphony of rebellion until they reached the grand staircase. There, amidst the swirling chaos, stood Genevieve, a beacon of determination and leadership. Her eyes burned with fervour as she rallied the Brides, her words cutting through the pandemonium.

"Sisters! Today we rise against the shackles that bind us. No more will we endure the torment of these monsters. Today, we fight for our freedom!" Genevieve's voice soared above the chaos, infusing the air with an electrifying energy.

Helena and Nikolai joined the throng of Brides, their eyes fixed on Genevieve. The rebellious spirit she had cultivated over months had ignited a spark that now blazed into a raging fire of defiance. Ravenna, a force of unbridled determination, appeared at the forefront. With a powerful swing, she shattered the door to Edward's office. The Brides erupted into triumphant cheers, the collective roaring a proclamation of their resolve.

"Hurrah! Hurrah!" The chants echoed through the halls, a thunderous declaration of rebellion that reverberated off the walls of the Nest. The vampires were now faced with an uprising that had been carefully orchestrated, a symphony of revolt led by the fierce determination of Genevieve.

"Today, we reclaim our lives! Today, we fight for those we've lost! Today, we stand together and declare our freedom!" Genevieve's rallying cry reached its zenith, her words carrying the weight of the collective pain and longing of every Bride.

As the hurrahs echoed, the Brides surged forward, a tidal wave of resistance crashing against the oppressive forces that had held them captive for far too long. The Nest, once a fortress of nightmares, had become the stage for a rebellion that would forever alter its dark legacy.

A molotov soared through the air, leaving a trail of flames as it arced toward Edward's office. Ravenna, living up to her name as the firebird, hoped to flush out the vampires who sought refuge within. But the act, executed with the fervor that defined her, had dire consequences.

"Ravenna, no!" Genevieve's voice sliced through the chaos, an anguished plea that seemed to slow down time itself. But the molotov crashed through the shattered door and ignited the hidden cache of flammable substances within.

A moment of deafening silence followed, a heartbeat suspended in the air. Then, an explosive burst of flames erupted from Edward's office, consuming everything in its voracious hunger. The fire roared to life, tendrils of orange and red licking the air with an insatiable appetite.

Caught in the inferno, Ravenna, the firebird, was flung backward, a human comet descending to the floor. The flames embraced her, becoming a cloak of searing agony. The hothead who had always rushed headlong into danger was now engulfed by the very fire she had unleashed.

Genevieve's eyes widened in horror, and time seemed to stretch as the reality of the moment sank in. Ravenna, the impulsive force of the rebellion, thrashed amidst the flames, her silhouette dancing with the cruel and chaotic rhythm of the fire. The sight was both stunning and heart-wrenching, a sudden and unexpected death in the midst of their uprising.

Helena, frozen in disbelief, stared at the inferno before her. The roaring flames reflected in her widened eyes, mirroring the chaotic dance of destruction. As the shock began to wear off, horror set in. The screams of the dying firebird reverberated in the air, each cry a poignant reminder of the price paid for rebellion.

In the midst of the pandemonium, Helena's gaze fell upon a glint on the floor amidst the wreckage. A knife, seemingly untouched by the flames, lay there, a silent witness to the unfolding tragedy.

Instinctively, she reached down, her fingers closing around the hilt. The blade felt cool against her trembling hand.

Her attention shifted back to Ravenna, whose thrashing silhouette was becoming indistinct in the engulfing blaze. A surge of determination replaced the shock on Helena's face. In a heartbeat decision, she pulled her arm back like drawing a bowstring, the knife gripped firmly. The blade felt cool against her trembling hand.

With a forceful throw, the knife sailed through the fiery chaos, cutting through the air with deadly precision. Time seemed to slow as it found its mark, striking Ravenna through the head. The blade ended the firebird's torment mercifully, bringing an abrupt silence to her cries. Helena's breath caught as she watched the life leave Ravenna's eyes, an unexpected mix of sorrow and relief flooding her.

The room, now a battlefield of fire and shadows, held a moment of eerie stillness. The flames, momentarily subdued by the unexpected turn, cast flickering shadows that danced across the faces of the surviving rebels. Helena stood amidst the devastation, her hand still outstretched, the knife now a symbol of both desperation and deliverance.

The rebellion had claimed one of its own, but Helena, in an act of grim necessity, had forged her own mark on the turbulent course of events. The firebird's sacrifice, though unintended, had left an indelible scar on the rebellion, forever etched into the hearts of those who survived the blazing ordeal. Ravenna, the firebird, had lived her compulsive life and, in a moment of compulsive mistake, had taken down many vampires in doing so.

Edward's maniacal laughter echoed through the chaos, a dissonant symphony of madness. His eyes glinted with the gleeful insanity of a man unhinged. The news of Ravenna's sacrifice seemed to fuel the flames of his delirium.
"Why did she do that?" he mocked, wiping tears from his eyes as he chuckled. "I wasn't even in the room... dumb, impulsive bitch!" His laughter intensified, and the scene became surreal, the mad conductor revelling in the discord he orchestrated.
As Edward approached Nikolai and Helena, the air grew heavier with tension. Edward revealed in the knowledge that Nikolai, bound by the sire bond, could not harm him. Panic clawed at Helena's throat as she scanned the chaotic surroundings, searching for a weapon, an escape.

In the midst of the turmoil, a voice cut through the madness. "Nikolai, take Helena away from here!" It was Genevieve, descending the stairs with purpose, wielding a sword in hand. Her eyes blazed with determination, and her voice, a rallying cry in the midst of chaos, pierced through the bedlam.

Nikolai seized the moment. Ignoring Edward's taunts, he grabbed Helena's arm and pulled her away from the impending danger. As they retreated, Genevieve faced Edward with a steely gaze, ready to confront the puppeteer orchestrating their suffering. The rebellion, though battered, remained unbroken, and Genevieve was determined to lead the charge against the tyrant who revealed in their torment.

The clash between Genevieve and Edward unfolded like a dark ballet on the grand staircase, the chaos of rebellion swirling around them like a malevolent storm. Flames roared, casting flickering shadows that danced with the rhythm of their violent confrontation.

"You always were a headstrong fool, Genevieve," Edward sneered, his voice echoing in the chaos. "Did you really think you could challenge me and live?"

Genevieve's eyes blazed with defiance. "I won't live as your puppet any longer, Edward. This ends today."

Their blades clashed with a symphony of ringing steel, the echoes punctuating their bitter exchange. The grand staircase became a battleground, the very heart of the rebellion's desperate stand.

"You were mine once, Genevieve," Edward taunted, his blows fueled by a mixture of sadistic pleasure and lingering affection. "You betrayed me, and now you'll pay the price."

Genevieve parried his strikes with a grace born from years of rebellion. "You betrayed yourself, Edward. Love turned to tyranny, and I'll be the instrument of your downfall."

The intensity of their conflict intensified, a whirlwind of flashing steel and raging emotions. As the flames licked at the edges of their battlefield, the two former lovers fought with a ferocity that mirrored the depth of their shared history.

In a sudden revelation that froze the chaos, Genevieve's eyes bore into Edward's weakened form. "You wonder why you've grown so weak, Edward? It's because of me."

Edward's face contorted in confusion, and a hint of fear flickered in his eyes.

"I've been poisoning you, slowly sapping your strength," Genevieve declared with a chilling calmness. "It's time for you to face the consequences."

Seizing the opportunity, Genevieve lunged forward, catching Edward off guard. Her blade found its mark, swiftly severing his head from his body. Edward's eyes widened in shock, his voice silenced forever.

The grand staircase fell into a stunned silence. Genevieve, victorious but mortally wounded, stood over the fallen despot. With her last breath, she proclaimed, "The era of Bride slavery has ended."

Her body, battered and broken, succumbed to the injuries inflicted during the fierce battle. Genevieve collapsed, lifeless, her sacrifice marking the end of a chapter in the dark history of the Nest. The rebels, witnessing the demise of their tormentor, stood in awe of the fallen heroine who had led them to freedom.

The tumultuous echoes of the rebellion resonated through the air as Nikolai led the shell-shocked Helena away from the blazing ruins of the Nest. They moved through the shadows, away from the bloodshed and chaos that had engulfed the once-feared fortress.

As they reached a point where the flickering flames and distant cries seemed like a distant nightmare, Nikolai turned back to survey the burning remnants of their captivity. The Nest, once a symbol of their torment, now lay in ruins, consumed by the fires of liberation.

Turning her gaze from the burning structure, Helena's knees buckled, and she sank to the ground. Overwhelmed by a flood of emotions—relief, grief, and the weight of newfound freedom—she cried. Tears streamed down her face as the reality of their triumph and the sacrifices made for it settled upon her. Nikolai knelt beside her, offering a comforting presence. He knew the journey ahead would be arduous, but for the first time in years, hope blossomed in the ashes of their rebellion.

As the sounds of the raging rebellion continued to echo in the distance, Helena wept for the past, for the fallen, and for the uncertain future that awaited. The night air carried their shared sorrow and the collective relief of those who had dared to defy the chains that bound them.

And so, in the aftermath of the chaos, Helena and Nikolai remained on the outskirts of the once-dreaded Nest, gazing back at the flames that marked the end of an era and the beginning of a new, uncertain chapter in their lives.

Chapter Fourteen

A New Home

The first light of dawn painted the sky with hues of pink and orange as Nikolai and Helena stood hand-in-hand, overlooking the smouldering ruins of the once imposing Nest. The air was thick with the acrid scent of burning debris, a stark contrast to the freedom they had fought so hard to attain. Nikolai, with a heavy heart, turned to Helena, concern etched across his face. "We should find Violet and leave before more vampires arrive," he suggested, his voice laced with urgency. However, Helena's gaze was distant, her thoughts consumed by the chaos of the rebellion and the absence of Violet. A knot tightened in her chest as she realised she hadn't seen her since the fire had erupted. Panic seized her, and she frantically scanned the charred remnants of the Nest.
"Violet..." she whispered, the name escaping her lips like a desperate plea.

Nikolai, sensing Helena's distress, gently squeezed her hand. "We'll find her, Helena. We have to search the ruins; she might be hiding somewhere."

Tears welled up in Helena's eyes as she blamed herself for letting Violet slip away during the tumult of the escape. She collapsed to her knees, the weight of guilt and fear pressing down on her. Nikolai knelt beside her, wrapping his arms around her in a comforting embrace.

"It's not your fault," he murmured softly, trying to console her. "We'll search every inch of this place until we find her. She's strong, Helena. She's survived this long."

With a determined nod, Nikolai helped Helena to her feet. Together, hand in hand, they embarked on the heartbreaking task of scouring the ruined Nest in search of the missing Violet. The rising sun cast long shadows over the destruction, illuminating their path as they clung to hope in the face of uncertainty.

The frantic search through the rubble reached a crescendo as Nikolai and Helena tirelessly dug through the debris, their voices echoing Violet's name. Just as despair began to claw at their hearts, a faint cough pierced the air, drawing their attention.

From a hidden cellar entrance emerged Violet, dishevelled and covered in soot, but miraculously unharmed. The sight of her brought tears to Helena's eyes, and she rushed forward, embracing Violet in a tight, tearful hug.

"Violet! You're safe!" Helena exclaimed, her voice a mix of joy and relief.

Nikolai, too, couldn't contain his emotions. He swept Violet into his arms, holding her close as if afraid she might vanish. "I was so worried. Thank the stars you're alright," he whispered, pressing a kiss to her forehead.

Violet, in turn, clung to Nikolai, her eyes filled with gratitude and affection. "I thought I lost you both," she admitted, her voice choked with emotion.

Helena wiped away tears, smiling through the haze of emotions. "We're a family, Violet. We look out for each other."

Nikolai guided them away from the wreckage, his arms wrapped protectively around both Helena and Violet. They walked towards a sleek black limousine that had survived the chaos. Nikolai opened the door, ushering them inside, and the three of them shared a moment of quiet relief.

As the limousine sped away from the destroyed manor, leaving behind the remnants of their painful past, the bond between Nikolai, Helena, and Violet strengthened. The weight of their shared ordeal hung in the air, but so did the promise of a new beginning, a chance to rebuild their lives free from the shackles of the Nest.

Nikolai's secluded childhood manor stood as a refuge, hidden deep within the embrace of the forest. As the grand gothic house came into view, untouched by the chaos that had plagued the Nest, it exuded an air of forgotten elegance and an essence of a perfect nuclear family.
Nikolai led Helena and Violet through the imposing front doors, their creaking hinges echoing through the quiet halls. Dust motes danced in the filtered sunlight, creating an ethereal atmosphere. The manor seemed to hold memories of a time long past, a time when Nikolai was human, and the idea of family was something cherished.
"I haven't been here in years," Nikolai admitted, a hint of nostalgia in his voice. "But it still feels like home."

He guided them through the grand foyer, showcasing rooms filled with antique furniture and faded tapestries that told tales of the manor's storied past. Each step seemed to unravel a piece of Nikolai's history, and yet, the manor held an eerie stillness, as if time had frozen within its walls.

The trio wandered through the echoing corridors, discovering forgotten rooms that held the promise of a renewed life. A cosy library with shelves filled with weathered books, a sunlit conservatory that overlooked the sprawling garden, and a majestic dining hall with a long table that seemed ready for a family gathering.

Nikolai's gaze lingered on the surroundings, and a bittersweet smile played on his lips. "This place was meant for a family. Maybe... maybe we can make it one again."

Helena, Violet, and Nikolai spent the day trying to restore a semblance of normalcy to the manor. They explored the overgrown garden, shared stories in front of a crackling fireplace, and even attempted to cook a family dinner together. Laughter and warmth filled the air, a stark contrast to the dark memories of the Nest.

As night fell, they gathered in the library, surrounded by the soft glow of flickering candles. Nikolai looked at Helena and Violet, a newfound sense of purpose in his eyes. "Here, we can start anew. No more shadows of the past. Just us, a family."

Helena and Violet exchanged glances, the weight of their shared experiences lifting, if only for a moment. In the quiet embrace of the manor, they began to weave the threads of a family, forging bonds that transcended the trials they had faced. The secluded manor in the heart of the forest held the promise of a new beginning, a sanctuary where they could redefine what family meant to them.

Chapter Fifteen

In the end

The grand dining hall was adorned with antique furniture and tapestries, the atmosphere warm with the soft glow of candles. The flickering light cast gentle shadows on the polished wooden table, where Helena, Nikolai, and Violet were gathered for dinner.

Nikolai, dressed in elegant attire that befitted the grandeur of his secluded manor, presided at the head of the table. He carved the roast with precision, the rich aroma filling the air. The table was adorned with an array of dishes, a feast fit for a celebration.

Helena, seated beside Nikolai, wore a serene smile that masked the inner turmoil she felt. Despite the façade of happiness, the ghostly memory of her recent illness lingered in the recesses of her mind. She glanced at Violet, who sat across from her, a vision of youth and vitality. The young girl's eyes sparkled with affection and gratitude.

Violet, her hair cascading in waves around her shoulders, looked at Helena with genuine warmth. "Pass the potatoes, Mother?" she asked, her voice a melody that resonated with the semblance of familial bliss.

Nikolai obliged, a proud fatherly smile playing on his lips. The laughter of the trio echoed through the hall, creating an illusion of normalcy in the midst of their hidden struggles. Helena couldn't help but savour these fleeting moments of happiness, even if they were built upon the fragile foundation of their intertwined fates. As the conversation flowed, tales of shared memories and laughter intertwined with the clinking of cutlery against fine china. The warmth in the room, however, couldn't dispel the haunting shadows that lingered in Helena's gaze. She knew that their idyllic family tableau was a fragile veneer masking the uncertainty of her own mortality.

The echoes of laughter mingled with the bittersweet taste of the meal, creating a poignant symphony that resonated through the grandeur of the manor. In this fleeting moment, as they found solace in each other's company, the spectre of their past and the uncertainties of the future danced in the background, waiting for the next act to unfold.

The grandeur of the manor dimmed as evening descended, and a hushed pallor settled over the rooms. Helena, despite her attempts to maintain an air of normalcy, couldn't escape the encroaching grip of her weakening body. She sighed, the weight of her weariness evident in each breath.

As the flickering candles cast shadows around the room, Nikolai approached Helena with an earnest plea in his eyes. "Helena, please," he implored, his voice tinged with desperation. "Let me turn you into a vampire. I can't bear to see you suffer like this."

Helena, wearing a simple nightgown that spoke of vulnerability, met Nikolai's gaze with a mixture of gratitude and determination. She placed a gentle hand on his cheek, her touch a silent reassurance. "Nikolai, turning me into a vampire would be a gift with strings attached. I would lose the essence of what makes me human. I don't want to sacrifice that, not even for immortality."

Nikolai's eyes mirrored the conflict within him, torn between the desire to grant Helena relief and the respect for her wishes. He nodded reluctantly, the weight of his love for her evident in every gesture. "I just want you to be free from pain, Helena. I can't bear to see you like this."

She smiled weakly, acknowledging his concern. "I know, Nikolai. But my humanity is what makes me who I am. I want to hold on to that for as long as I can."

With a tender touch, Helena withdrew from Nikolai's embrace and made her way to their shared bedroom. The softness of her nightgown brushed against her skin, a stark contrast to the complexity of emotions swirling within her. As she lay down, the weariness in her bones echoed the toll her condition had taken on her.

Closing her eyes, Helena sought solace in the fleeting respite that sleep offered. The room, bathed in the gentle glow of moonlight, witnessed the quiet struggle of a woman determined to cling to her humanity amidst the encroaching shadows of vampiric inevitability. The manor, once a sanctuary, held secrets that lingered in the silent spaces between heartbeats, as the weight of the night pressed on, full of both dreams and unspoken fears.

The moonlight filtered through the curtains, casting a silvery glow on Helena's sleeping form. Unbeknownst to her, a shadowy figure approached with a mixture of desperation and madness in his eyes. Nikolai, driven to the brink by the fear of losing Helena, couldn't bear the thought of her suffering any longer.

As Nikolai leaned over her, his fangs ready to pierce her neck, Helena's instincts kicked in. A surge of adrenaline coursed through her weakened body as she woke abruptly, the world around her a blurry haze. Reacting on pure instinct, she fought against Nikolai's grasp, the struggle fueled by the last reserves of her fading strength.

In a desperate reach, Helena's trembling hand found the familiar hilt of Serena's silver dagger. The ribbon, once a symbol of camaraderie and shared history, now served a darker purpose. With a determined thrust, she plunged the dagger into Nikolai's heart, the metallic clang echoing in the silent room.

A strangled gasp escaped Nikolai as his eyes widened in shock. The fervour that had fueled him moments ago transformed into agony, and he crumpled to the floor. Helena, panting and bewildered by her own actions, stared at the lifeless body before her. The room, once a sanctuary, now held the echoes of a tragedy that unfolded in the dead of night.

Haunted by the weight of what she had just done, Helena stumbled out of the room and into the dimly lit corridor. The reality of her solitude set in, and her eyes wandered to Violet's bedroom. The guilt etched across her face deepened as she realised the magnitude of her actions—she had not only lost the man she loved but had irreversibly altered Violet's world.

Helena leaned against the wall, catching her breath as the weight of the night pressed on her shoulders. The moon witnessed the aftermath of a desperate struggle, leaving behind a woman who had, in a moment of self-preservation, severed the ties that bound her to both love and guilt. The manor, silent witness to the tumultuous events, held Helena in its shadows as she grappled with the consequences of an unforgiving choice.

With the cold night air biting at her face, Helena hastily threw on her coat, the fabric rustling like the distant whisper of leaves in the wind. The crimson-stained handkerchief, a testament to the turmoil within, was clutched tightly in her hand. Determination flickered in her eyes as she stepped out into the darkness, guided only by the moon's silvery glow.

The night embraced her, and Helena's footsteps echoed in the silence of the sprawling forest surrounding Nikolai's secluded manor. Each step, though weighed down by the burden of recent events, carried a flicker of hope. In her heart, she harboured a conviction—a belief that somewhere, somehow, she would find Lucy Sparks, the beacon of her undying hope.

The rhythmic beat of her heart resonated with the cadence of the night as Helena navigated the twists and turns of the forest paths. The path ahead was unknown, shrouded in uncertainty, but her determination refused to waver. The occasional cough, punctuated by the metallic taste of blood, served as a stark reminder of the fragility of her existence.

As Helena ventured deeper into the woods, the moonlight cast an ethereal glow on her path. Shadows danced among the trees, and the night seemed to hold its breath, awaiting the resolution of a story that had unfolded with the darkness as its witness. Each step brought her closer to the unknown, to the hope she clung to like a lifeline.

In the vast expanse of the forest, Helena's figure became a solitary silhouette against the night. Her journey, a quest for something beyond the grasp of a world entangled in shadows, unfolded beneath the canopy of ancient trees. The echo of her footsteps harmonised with the night's symphony, a melody that resonated with both loss and the enduring flame of hope.

With every heartbeat, Helena pressed forward, driven by the undying hope that Lucy Sparks, a connection to her past, awaited her somewhere in the unknown. The night held its secrets, but Helena, draped in her coat and carrying the weight of her choices, moved forward—a lone figure on a journey guided by the elusive promise of a brighter dawn.

Epilogue

It doesn't end so simply

Word of the Blood Brides' daring uprising at the Nest manor spread quickly amongst the settlements. The tale of their bravery against such imposing oppressors lit a flame of inspiration for change.

Soon, stories circulated of copycat rebellions breaking out across the land. Servants revolted against their vampire masters. Victims fought back against their tormentors. Small cells of resistance coordinated more ambitious attacks against regime strongholds. The fire at the Nest had only been the first spark. Now the flame of revolution was catching and spreading. The Brides' bold stand gave oppressed humans everywhere newfound courage to envision a life free from blood bondage.

Of course, the vampire overlords did not relinquish their power so easily. They quashed many uprisings with ruthless force, determined to maintain control. Rivers of blood were spilled in the name of liberty.

But the spirit of resistance endured and evolved, fueled by the martyred Brides' inspirational memory. Their revolt had broken the aura of invincibility around the vampire regime. They proved the immortals could be defied and defeated, even destroyed.

So while the Brides' specific fight may have ended, their larger impact rippled outward for years to come. Their brazen refusal to surrender lit the fuse on a change that would one day topple the rotten kingdom built on their blood, pain and sacrifice.

This was just the beginning...of the end. Their bold uprising marks the first page in the story of a revolution that would echo through history. The Brides showed the world that even the darkest night must yield to the coming dawn.

Acknowledgements

To my very own rebellion

First and foremost, I want to thank L.J. Smith, whose Vampire Diaries books first introduced me to the enthralling world of vampires as a teenager. Those stories sparked a lifelong love of gothic lore and romance.

Of course, credit is also due to Bram Stoker, whose Dracula cemented vampires in the public imagination and laid the groundwork for so much of what came after. His chilling portrayal shaped the darker side of vampire fiction.

I'm grateful to my friends who have indulged my enthusiasm for shows like Vampire Diaries over the years. Our spirited discussions about vampire romances, gothic heroines, and sinister villains inspired me more than they know.

Thanks to my father for exposing me to the more frightening vampires in film and television, reminding me of their monstrous roots. You taught me how vampires could be more than just charismatic immortal lovers.

Most of all, I want to thank my late mother, who nurtured my passion for writing from an early age. Your unwavering support gave me the courage to pursue this passion and tell the tragic tale of the Blood Brides. I hope I've made you proud.

And finally, thank you dear readers for taking a chance on this book and allowing me to transport you into its dark, melancholic world. It was a privilege to share the plight of the Brides with you. I appreciate you joining their rebellion.

Yours in solidarity,

Mckenzy Dominy

This story is far from over...

Printed in Great Britain
by Amazon